John B Bagshawe

The catechism illustrated by passages from the Holy Scriptures

with an appendix and notes

John B Bagshawe

The catechism illustrated by passages from the Holy Scriptures
with an appendix and notes

ISBN/EAN: 9783741189876

Manufactured in Europe, USA, Canada, Australia, Japa

Cover: Foto ©Andreas Hilbeck / pixelio.de

Manufactured and distributed by brebook publishing software
(www.brebook.com)

John B Bagshawe

The catechism illustrated by passages from the Holy Scriptures

PREFACE.

THIS compilation is intended to assist our children in
acquiring a better knowledge of the Holy Scripture.
The Catholic Church has always loved the Written Word
of God. In the ages of persecution her children thought
it their duty to preserve the Holy Scripture from profanation, if necessary at the risk of their lives. Many
martyrs suffered death rather than let their sacred books
fall into pagan hands. When the bishops later on were
able publicly to meet in Council, they placed the book of
the Holy Scriptures on a throne in the midst of them. In
the public offices of the Church those marks of respect
to the book of the Gospels were introduced which we see
used in our own days. When evil times arrived, and the
new framework of society was broken up, it was nothing
but the constant care of the Church which preserved to
us the Holy Scriptures. In the middle ages—emphati-
cally the ages of faith—men thought it an honour to
spend their lives in copying them. They deemed no
amount of time and labour too great to spend in enriching
and beautifying those volumes which contained the Word
of God. As they had these volumes in their hands, so
did they also bear them in their hearts. Night and day
you might have heard the praises of God sung in the
words of Holy Scripture in a hundred monasteries.
Every monk was supposed to know by heart the whole
Psalter, and to carry out most literally the precept given

by God to the Jews, "And these words, which I command thee this day, shall be in thy heart : and thou shalt tell them to thy children, and thou shalt meditate upon them sitting in thy house, and walking on thy journey, sleeping and rising" (Deut. vi. 6). Every one, who was educated at all, was familiar with the language of the Scriptures, so that the very words and phrases of Scripture had insinuated themselves into every kind of writing on indifferent subjects. Dr. Maitland, in the life-like account he gives of those times, tells us that the only way to understand the meaning of middle-age writers in difficult places is by referring to the language used in the Bible.

This shows us what is the instinct of the Catholic Church about the Holy Scriptures. The time did indeed come when restrictions were found necessary. When every artisan began to think it his business to find a faith for himself—and a confusion of tongues was the consequence ; when men were "carried away by every wind of doctrine," and the "unlearned and unstable" had come upon those things "hard to be understood" which, S. Peter tells us, they "wrest to their own destruction" (2 S. Pet. iii. 16) ; then, indeed, the Church found it necessary, in some degree, to keep the Bible from the hands of those who were using it in such a manner as to profane the Holy Word of God and to endanger their own souls. The Church, therefore, made certain wise regulations about reading the Scriptures, intended to direct us how to make them, as the Apostle says, "profitable to teach, to reprove, to correct, to instruct in justice : that the man of God may be perfect, furnished to every good work" (2 Tim. iii. 16) ; at the same time commanding and exhorting her children to apply themselves earnestly, under proper guidance, to the

study of them.—*Conc. Trid. Sess. 5. c. 1 de Refor.* Almost
in our own times we find Pope Pius VI. declaring that
the faithful should be "excited to the reading of the
Holy Scriptures; for these are the most abundant
sources, which ought to be left open to every one, to
draw from them purity of morals, and of doctrine, to
eradicate the errors which are so widely disseminated in
these corrupt times;" and praising those who had put
them before the faithful "in the language of their country," and in a manner "suitable to every one's capacity."
—*Letter of Pope Pius VI. to the Archbishop of Florence.*

It appears to me that the present is especially a time
when Catholics are bound to have a proper knowledge
of the Holy Scriptures and to display a great devotion
towards them. The distinguishing heresy of the day is
an attack on Revelation generally, and in particular on
the Inspiration of the Bible, which ought to bring out
a proportionate spirit of loyalty towards it in the
Church. On the other hand, the danger to be appre-
hended to Faith, from an extensive use of the Bible,
seems in a great measure to have died out with the
decay of the principle of private judgment exercised on
Scripture. This principle itself has been weighed in the
balance and found wanting. All the evil that it could
do has long since been done. The errors to which it
gave rise have long since been confuted, so that it now
seems more than ever a duty incumbent upon all Catholics to make themselves familiar with the Word of God,
and to draw as plentifully as possible from those fountains which the Spirit of God has opened to them.

Of course it is not to be supposed that any adequate
knowledge of Holy Scripture can be acquired by reading
a small collection of texts; but still I think that children
would get a foundation for this kind of knowledge, and

a taste for it, by looking for and learning a certain number of striking passages, and becoming acquainted with their application to the different doctrines taught by the Church.

The primary object of this book is not controversial, but devotional; that is, not to make our children sharp controversialists, but to store their minds with some of the grand thoughts and beautiful expressions which occur in the Inspired Writings, so that the truth of religion may not be to them naked forms of words, but may be associated with beautiful and devotional thoughts likely to come back to them in times of trial. I say the *primary* object because, of course, the principal texts, which will be useful to those who are called upon to give an account of their Faith, will be found in their places.

I have called the book the "Catechism *Illustrated*," because it does not attempt or profess to *prove* the Catholic Faith from Scripture. To do so would be entirely contrary to the spirit of the Church. Every Catholic knows that the doctrines of the Catholic Church are independent of Scripture; that is to say, that the Church teaches from the plenitude of the power committed to her; that she did so from the beginning, before the New Testament was written—centuries, indeed, before the Bible was collected into its present form; and that she would have done so in precisely the same manner had they never been written. For example, every Catholic knows that the Faith of the Church about the Holy Eucharist would have been precisely what it is, had it pleased God that not one of the passages relating to It ever had been written; and, therefore, that these passages, however clear they may be, cannot properly be referred to as the ground of the Church's teaching.

A Catholic looks upon the Church and the Holy

Scriptures as two distinct and independent sources of religious knowledge, both coming from God—the one illustrating and explaining indeed, but not the mere echo of the other, dependent on it for authority.

I have also indulged in the hope that this book may be useful to Protestants. I believe the Catechism to be one of the best possible books of controversy, to those, at least, who are inquiring with a real desire to find the truth. It is impossible for any one to have a reasonably accurate knowledge of the Catholic Faith without being brought nearer to it, especially when put in the way of seeing how closely it agrees, not with half a dozen isolated passages, but with the whole teaching and spirit of the Scriptures.

I must observe that, as the object of the book is not *controversy*, but *illustration*, it will sometimes happen that texts are chosen which would not be legitimate in strict controversy; that is, texts the words of which admit of a different explanation from the one suggested, or which, from the context, appear to have been originally used in a different sense. I have subjoined a few words on the canon of Scripture ; and also a list of the different books given in the Catholic and Protestant Bible, with a view to assisting such Protestants as may wish to verify any of the passages quoted.

I must conclude by asking the indulgence of the reader for the many omissions which he will certainly find in this little book ; and by hoping that it may please God to make it a means of increasing the knowledge and love of His Holy Word, and of leading souls to that Faith taught by His Church.

RICHMOND,
Feast of SS. Peter and Paul, 1870.

INTRODUCTION.

ON THE CANON OF SCRIPTURE.

THE canon of Scripture received by the Catholic Church is that laid down by the Council of Trent. The word "canon" means *rule*, and here it is used to signify the catalogue of works which the Church receives as inspired by God. Let us consider (1) the process by which such a canon of Scripture was arrived at ; (2) the authority by which it became binding on the consciences of Christians ; (3) what this canon actually is.

The Scriptures were written, not as one whole, but in the shape of a number of different treatises, which, so far from making parts of a whole, were written by different authors, at different times, addressed to different people, and for widely varying objects. Many books were addressed to small bodies, and, in the first instance, were not *intended* for all mankind. For example, most of S. Paul's epistles were written to the people of some particular city, for some special purpose, and were intended to be read only by the Christians residing there, and perhaps by those of the neighbouring towns. It must, therefore, have been many years before all the different parts of the Scripture could have been even known to Christians generally, and many more years before the Christian world could have been able to form any decided opinion on their genuineness and authority. We find, accordingly, in the early Church a great uncertainty about the Scriptures. Portions of the New Testament were almost unknown in some countries, whilst apocryphal writings of all descriptions, highly coloured accounts of our Lord's life and miracles, and of the teaching of His apostles, sprang up every where and appeared to carry with them more or less authority. How was all this confusion to end? It was obviously beyond the power of any individual, however learned and holy he might be, to pronounce in such a case as this. It could only end by the intervention of an authority having a right to speak in the Name of God. Nothing less than a Divine authority could venture to pronounce on the Divine Inspiration of God's Word. Accordingly, in due time, that is, when the knowledge of Scripture was sufficiently diffused, the Church did pronounce, and that decision has been final. In the year of our Lord 397 the Council of Carthage, following the tradition of the Church and the teaching of other councils which had preceded it, published a rule or canon of Scripture which has been the canon of the Christian Church ever since. The Council of Trent did little more than re-enact the same canon.

About three hundred years ago, when this canon had been for eleven centuries acknowledged by all Christians, Protestants thought fit to reconsider it, and to leave out some books both of the Old and the New Testament. On what principle they did so is not very apparent. As they had rejected the idea of a Church teaching with authority from God,—the one principle on which Christians had hitherto received the Bible,—it is not easy to see how they could find a firm basis for a decision on the Holy Scriptures ; and, accordingly, we are not much surprised to find that they could not agree amongst themselves, and that the Lutherans adopted one canon and the Calvinists another. The unfortunate result, however, is that, to the present day, Protestants, on the faith of the judgment of certain private individuals at the time of the Reformation, reject some portions of the Word of God. I have thought it desirable, therefore, to give a list of the books comprised in the canon of Scripture, showing the different names by which they are sometimes known, and marking those omitted by Protestants.

In the Anglican version the Psalms are divided and numbered in a manner which slightly differs from that in use in the Catholic Church. In each version there are 150 Psalms.

The two versions correspond until the ninth Psalm ; but the ninth Psalm of the Vulgate includes the ninth and tenth of the English version. The consequence of this is that from

Psalm ix. to Psalm cxiii. the number given to each Psalm in the latter is *one above* that given in the Vulgate. Thus, the Miserere, Psalm l., is called in the English version, Psalm li. Psalm cxiii. of the Vulgate contains Psalms cxiv. and cxv. of the Anglican version, whilst, on the other hand, Psalms cxiv. and cxv. of the Vulgate are both comprised in Psalm cxvi. of the other version. Psalm cxvii., therefore, of the English version corresponds to Psalm cxvi. of the Vulgate ; and so the Psalms in the former continue to be one higher in number till Psalm cxlvii. of the English version, which includes Psalms cxlvi. and cxlvii. of the Vulgate, so that Psalms cxlviii., cxlix., and cl. correspond in the two versions. There is also a slight difference in the numbering of the verses in some of the Psalms. It may be added that there is more variation in the translations of the Psalms than in those of most other parts of Scripture ; probably on account of their highly poetical nature, and on account of the devotional use made of them in the Church for so many centuries. It may be well to observe that a great many of the Scripture names are written and pronounced in two different ways— one taken from the Latin form of the Hebrew name, the other from the original. For the former it may be said that it is the form which has been almost exclusively used in the Christian Church for eighteen centuries ; for the latter, that it is supposed more nearly to approach the name as actually used. In what degree either pronunciation resembles that in use in the time (say) of King David may be rather a matter of speculation.

LIST OF BOOKS OF SCRIPTURE.

Old Testament.

The Vulgate, or Catholic Version.				The Anglican Version.
Genesis	otherwise called	. .		Genesis.
Exodus	,,	,,	. .	Exodus.
Leviticus	,,	,,	. .	Leviticus.
Numbers	,,	,,	. .	Numbers.
Deuteronomy	,,	,,	. .	Deuteronomy.
Josue	,,	,,	. .	Joshua.
Judges	,,	,,	. .	Judges.
Ruth	,,	,,	. .	Ruth.
1 Kings	,,	,,	. .	1 Samuel.

Pentateuch. {Genesis, Exodus, Leviticus, Numbers, Deuteronomy}

2 Kings	otherwise called	. .	2 Samuel.
3 Kings	,, ,,	. .	1 Kings.
4 Kings	,, ,,	. .	2 Kings.
1 Paralipomenon	,, ,,	. .	1 Chronicles.
2 Paralipomenon	,, ,,	. .	2 Chronicles.
1 Esdras	,, ,,	. .	Ezra.
2 Esdras	,, ,,	. .	Nehemiah.
Tobias	,, ,,	. .	omitted.
Judith	,, ,,	. .	omitted.
Esther	,, ,,	. .	Esther.
Job	,, ,,	. .	Job.
Psalms	,, ,,	. .	Psalms.
Proverbs	,, ,,	. .	Proverbs.
Ecclesiastes, *abbrev.* Eccl.	,,	. .	Ecclesiastes.
Canticle of Canticles	,,	. .	Song of Solomon.
Wisdom	,, ,,	. •	omitted.
Ecclesiasticus, *abbrev.* Ecclus.		. .	omitted.

Greater Prophets.

Isaias	,, ,,	. .	Isaiah.
Jeremias	,, ,,	. .	Jeremiah.
Lamentations	,, ,,	. .	Lamentations.
Baruch	,, ,,	. .	omitted.
Ezechiel	,, ,,	. .	Ezekiel.
Daniel	,, ,,	. .	Daniel.

Lesser Prophets.

Osee	,, ,,	. .	Hosea.
Joel	,, ,,	. .	Joel.
Amos	,, ,,	. .	Amos.
Abdias	,, ,,	. .	Obadiah.
Jonas	,, ,,	. .	Jonah.
Micheas	,, ,,	. .	Micah.
Nahum	,, ,,	. .	Nahum.
Habacuc	,, ,,	. .	Habakkuk.
Sophonias	,, ,,	. .	Zephaniah.
Aggeus	,, ,,	. .	Haggai.
Zacharias	,, ,,	. .	Zechariah.
Malachias	,, ,,	. .	Malachi.
1 Machabees	,, ,,	. .	omitted.
2 Machabees	,, ,,	. .	omitted.

New Testament.

Gospels.

S. Matthew.
S. Mark.
S. Luke.
S. John.

Acts of the Apostles.
S. Paul to the Romans.
    ,,   Corinthians (1).

S. Paul to the Corinthians (2).
      ,,   Galatians.
      ,,   Ephesians.
      ,,   Philippians.
      ,,   Colossians.
      ,,   Thessalonians (1).
      ,,   Thessalonians (2).
      ,,   Timothy (1).
      ,,   Timothy (11).
      ,,   Titus.
      ,,   Philemon.
      ,,   Hebrews.
S. James.
1 S. Peter.
2 S. Peter.
1 S. John.
2 S. John.
3 S. John.
S. Jude.
Apocalypse, otherwise called Revelation.

THE CATECHISM ILLUSTRATED

———◆———

CHAPTER I.

Q. Who made you?
A. God.

God created man of the earth, and made him after His own image (*Ecclus.* xvii. 1).

Know ye that the Lord He is God : He made us, and not we ourselves. We are His people and the sheep of His pasture (*Ps.* xcix. 3).

Q. Why did God make you?
A. To know Him, love Him, and serve Him in this world, and to be happy with Him for ever in the next.

Now this is eternal life : that they may know Thee, the only true God, and Jesus Christ, whom Thou hast sent (*S. John* xvii. 3).

My son, give Me thy heart: and let thy eyes keep My ways (*Prov.* xxiii. 26).

For what have I in heaven? and besides Thee what do I desire upon earth? For Thee my flesh and my heart hath fainted away: Thou art the God of my heart, and the God that is my portion for ever (*Ps.* lxxii. 25).

By Thy ordinance the day goeth on : for all things serve Thee (*Ps.* cxviii. 91).

Serve ye the Lord with fear : and rejoice unto Him with trembling (*Ps.* ii. 11).

Fear not, Abram, I am thy protector, and thy reward exceeding great (*Gen.* xv. 1).

One thing I have asked of the Lord, this will I seek after; that I may dwell in the house of the Lord all the days of my life; that I may see the delight of the Lord, and visit His temple (*Ps.* xxvi. 4).

Q. To whose likeness did God make you?
A. To His own image and likeness.

And He said: Let us make man to our image and likeness (*Gen.* i. 26).

Q. Is this likeness in your body or in your soul?
A. In my soul.

Stripping yourselves of the old man with his deeds, and putting on the new, him who is renewed unto knowledge, according to the image of Him that created him (*Col.* iii. 9).

Q. How is your soul like to God?
A. Because my soul is a spirit and is immortal.

God is a Spirit, and they that adore Him, must adore Him in spirit and in truth (*S. John* iv. 24).
Now the Lord is a Spirit. And where the Spirit of the Lord is, there is liberty (2 *Cor.* iii. 17).

Q. What do you mean, when you say that your soul is immortal?
A. I mean that my soul can never die.

And fear ye not them that kill the body, and are not able to kill the soul: but rather fear Him that can destroy both soul and body into hell (*S. Matt.* x. 28).

Q. Of which must you take most care, of your body, or of your soul?
A. Of my soul: for Christ has said, " What doth it profit a man if he gain the whole world, and suffer the loss of his own soul?" (*Matt.* xvi. 26.)

Seek ye therefore first the kingdom of God, and His justice, and all these things shall be added unto you (*S. Matt.* vi. 33).
For whosoever will save his life, shall lose it; for he that shall lose his life for My sake, shall save it. For what is a man advantaged, if he gain the whole world, and lose himself, and cast away himself? (*S. Luke* ix. 24.)
The kingdom of heaven is like unto a treasure hidden in a field; which a man having found, hideth and for joy thereof goeth, and selleth all that he hath, and buyeth that field. Again the kingdom of heaven is like to a merchant seeking good

pearls : who when he had found one pearl of great price, went his way, and sold all that he had, and bought it (*S. Matt.* xiii. 44).

Lay not up to yourselves treasures on earth: where the rust and moth consume, and where thieves break through and steal. But lay up to yourselves treasures in heaven : where neither rust nor moth doth consume, and where thieves do not break through, nor steal (*S. Matt.* vi. 19).

And He spoke a similitude to them, saying : The land of a certain rich man brought forth plenty of fruits. And he thought within himself, saying : What shall I do, because I have no room where to bestow my fruits? And he said : This will I do : I will pull down my barns, and will build greater : and into them will I gather all things that are grown to me, and my goods. And I will say to my soul : Soul, thou hast much goods laid up for many years, take thy rest, eat, drink, make good cheer. But God said to him : Thou fool, this night do they require thy soul of thee ; and whose shall those things be which thou hast provided ? So is he that layeth up treasure for himself, and is not rich towards God (*S. Luke* xii. 16).

Q. What must you do to save your soul?

A. I must worship God by faith, hope, and charity ; that is, I must believe in Him, hope in Him, and love Him with my whole heart.

O the depth of the riches of the wisdom and of the knowledge of God ! How incomprehensible are His judgments, and how unsearchable His ways ! (*Rom.* xi. 23.)

For the weapons of our warfare are not carnal, but mighty to God unto the pulling down of fortifications, destroying counsels, and every height that exalteth itself against the knowledge of God, and bringing into captivity every understanding unto the obedience of Christ (2 *Cor.* x. 5).

For we are saved by hope. But hope that is seen, is not hope. For what a man seeth, why doth he hope for? But if we hope for that which we see not, we wait for it with patience (*Rom.* viii. 24).

In Thee, O Lord, have I hoped, let me never be confounded (*Ps.* xxx. 2).

Who then shall separate us from the love of Christ? shall tribulation? or distress? or famine? or nakedness? or danger? or persecution? or the sword? (*Rom.* viii. 35.)

If then you obey My commandments, which I command you this day, that you love the Lord your God, and serve Him with all your heart, and with all your soul: He will give to your land the early rain and the latter rain, that you may gather in your corn, and your wine, and your oil (*Deut.* xi. 13).

Q. What is faith?
A. It is to believe without doubting whatever God has revealed.

For whatsoever is born of God, overcometh the world: and this is the victory which overcometh the world, our faith. Who is he that overcometh the world, but he that believeth that Jesus is the Son of God? (1 *S. John* v. 4.)

But let him ask in faith, nothing wavering. For he that wavereth is like a wave of the sea, which is moved and carried about by the wind (*S. James* i. 6).

See here is water, what doth hinder me from being baptized? And Philip said: If thou believest with all thy heart thou mayst. And he answering, said: I believe that Jesus Christ is the Son of God (*Acts* viii. 36).

Q. Why must you be-

God is not as a man, that He

lieve whatever God has revealed ?

A. Because God is the very truth, and cannot deceive or be deceived.

Q. How are you to know what the things are which God has revealed?

A. By the testimony and authority of the Catholic Church, which Christ has appointed to teach all nations.

should lie, nor as the son of man, that He should be changed. Hath He said then, and will He not do? hath He spoken, and will He not fulfil? (*Num.* xxiii. 19.)

For His mercy is confirmed upon us: and the truth of the Lord remaineth for ever (*Ps.* cxvi. 2).

Necessity of Revelation.

And Jesus answering, said to him: Blessed art thou, Simon Barjona: because flesh and blood hath not revealed it to thee, but My Father who is in heaven (*S. Matt.* xvi. 17).

At that time Jesus answered and said: I confess to Thee, O Father, Lord of heaven and earth, because Thou hast hid these things from the wise and prudent, and hast revealed them to little ones (*S. Matt.* xi. 25).

And no one knoweth the Son, but the Father: neither doth any one know the Father, but the Son, and he to whom it shall please the Son to reveal Him (*S. Matt.* xi. 27).

Testimony of the Church.

But you shall receive the power of the Holy Ghost coming upon you, and you shall be witnesses unto Me in Jerusalem, and in all Judea, and Samaria, and even to the uttermost part of the earth (*Acts* i. 8).

This Jesus hath God raised again, whereof all we are witnesses (*Acts* ii. 33).

Authority of the Church.

He that heareth you, heareth Me: and he that despiseth you, despiseth Me. And he that despiseth Me, depiseth Him that sent Me (*S. Luke* x. 16).

Q. What are the chief

Hold the form of sound words

things which God has revealed?

A. Those which are contained in the Apostles' Creed.

Say the Apostles' Creed.

I believe in God the Father Almighty, Creator of Heaven and earth;—and in Jesus Christ, His only Son, our Lord;—Who was conceived by the Holy Ghost, born of the Virgin Mary;—suffered under Pontius Pilate, was crucified, dead and buried;—He descended into Hell;—the third day He rose again from the dead;—He ascended into Heaven; sitteth at the right hand of God the Father Almighty;—from thence He shall come to judge the living and the dead.

I believe in the Holy Ghost;—the Holy Catholic Church ; — the communion of Saints; —the forgiveness of sins; —the resurrection of the body;—and life everlasting. Amen.

Q. How is the Apostles' Creed divided?

A. Into twelve parts or articles.

First Article of the Creed.

Q. What is the first article of the Creed?

A. I believe in God the Father Almighty, Creator of Heaven and earth.

which thou hast heard of me, in faith, and in the love which is in Jesus Christ (2 *Tim.* i. 13).

For this cause I bow my knees to the Father of our Lord Jesus Christ, of whom all paternity in heaven and earth is named (*Eph.* iii. 14).

Q. What is God ?
A. God is the Supreme Spirit, who exists of Himself, and is infinite in all perfections.

Self-existence of God.

Moses said to God : Lo, I shall go to the children of Israel, and say to them : The God of your fathers hath sent me to you. If they should say to me : What is His name? what shall I say to them? God said to Moses : I AM WHO AM. He said : Thus shalt thou say to the children of Israel : HE WHO IS, hath sent me to you (*Exod.* iii. 13).

For as the Father hath life in Himself; so He hath given to the Son also to have life in Himself (*S. John* v. 26).

Abraham your father rejoiced that he might see My day : he saw it, and was glad. The Jews therefore said to Him : Thou art not yet fifty years old, and hast Thou seen Abraham? Jesus said to them : Amen, amen, I say to you, before Abraham was made, I am (*S. John* viii. 56).

Majesty of God.

Behold the Lord God shall come with strength, and His arm shall rule : behold His reward is with Him and His work is before Him. He shall feed His flock like a shepherd : He shall gather together the lambs with His arm, and shall take them up in His bosom, and He Himself shall carry them that are with young. Who hath measured the waters in the hollow of His hand, and weighed the heavens with His palm? Who hath poised with three fingers the bulk of the earth, and weighed the mountains in scales, and the hills in a balance? Who hath forwarded the spirit of the Lord? or who hath been His counsellor, and hath taught Him? With whom hath He consulted, and who hath instructed Him, and taught Him the path of justice, and taught Him knowledge, and showed Him the way of understanding? Behold the gentiles are as a drop of a bucket, and are counted as the smallest grain of a balance : behold the islands are as a little dust. And Libanus shall not be enough to burn, nor the beasts thereof sufficient for a burnt-offering. All nations are before Him as if they had no being at all, and are counted to Him as nothing, and vanity (*Isa.* xl. 10).

For great power always belonged to Thee alone : and who shall resist the strength of Thy arm? For the whole world before Thee is as the least grain of the balance, and as a drop of the morning dew, that falleth down upon the earth (*Wisd.* xi. 22).

He that liveth for ever created all things together. God only shall be justified, and He remaineth an invincible king for ever. Who is able to declare His works? For who shall search out His glorious acts? And who shall show forth the power of His majesty? or who shall be able to declare His mercy? (*Ecclus.* xviii. 1.)

For who shall say to Thee : What hast Thou done? or who shall withstand Thy judgment? or who shall come before Thee to be a revenger of wicked men? or who shall accuse Thee, if the nations perish, which Thou hast made? (*Wisd.* xii. 12.)

Goodness of God.

And behold one came and said to Him : Good Master, what good shall I do that I may have life everlasting?

Who said to him : Why askest thou Me concerning good? One is good, God (*S. Matt.* xix. 16).

But Thou, our God, art gracious and true, patient, and ordering all things in mercy. For if we sin, we are Thine, knowing Thy greatness : and if we sin not, we know that we are counted with Thee. For to know Thee is perfect justice : and to know Thy justice, and Thy power, is the root of immortality (*Wisd.* xv. 1).

What is man that Thou art mindful of him ? or the son of man that Thou visitest him ? (*Ps.* viii. 5.)

Q. Why is He called Almighty?

A. Because He can do all things : " With God all things are possible" (*Matt.* xix. 26).

Because no word shall be impossible with God (*S. Luke* i. 37).

He said to them : The things that are impossible with men, are possible with God (*S. Luke* xviii. 27).

Q. Why is He called Creator of Heaven and earth ?

A. Because He made Heaven and earth, and all things out of nothing, by His only word.

By the word of the Lord the heavens were established, and all the power of them by the spirit of His mouth (*Ps.* xxxii. 6).

For He spoke and they were made : He commanded and they were created (*Ps.* xxxii. 9).

Thou art worthy, O Lord our God, to receive glory, and honour, and power : because Thou hast created all things, and for Thy will they were, and have been created (*Apoc.* iv. 11).

And : Thou in the beginning, O Lord, didst found the earth : and the works of Thy hands are the heavens. They shall perish, but Thou shalt continue : and they shall all grow old as a garment. And as a vesture shalt Thou change them, and they shall be changed : but Thou art the self-same, and Thy years shall not fail (*Heb.* i. 10).

Thus saith the Lord : Heaven is My throne, and the earth My footstool : what is this house that you will build to Me ? and what is this place of My rest ? My hand made all these things, and all these things

were made, saith the Lord.   But to
whom shall I have respect, but to
him that is poor and little, and of a
contrite spirit, and that trembleth at
My words? (*Isa.* lxvi. 1.)

Where wast thou when I laid the
foundations of the earth? tell Me if
thou hast understanding.   Who hath
laid the measures thereof, if thou
knowest? or who hath stretched
the line upon it?   Upon what are
its bases grounded? or who laid the
corner stone thereof, when the
morning stars praised Me together,
and all the sons of God made a joy-
ful melody?   Who shut up the sea
with doors, when it broke forth as
issuing out of the womb: when I
made a cloud the garment thereof,
and wrapped it in a mist as in swaddling bands? I set My bounds around
it, and made it bars and doors; and
I said : Hitherto thou shalt come,
and shalt go no further, and here
thou shalt break thy swelling waves
(*Job* xxxviii. 4).

God the Preserver.

How great are Thy works, O Lord!
Thou hast made all things in wisdom : the earth is filled with Thy
riches.   So is this great sea, which
stretcheth wide its arms : there are
creeping things without number,
creatures little and great.   There
the ships shall go : this sea-dragon
which Thou hast formed to play
therein.   All expect of Thee that
Thou give them food in season.
What Thou givest to them they shall
gather up : when Thou openest Thy
hand, they shall all be filled with
good.   But if Thou turn away Thy
face, they shall be troubled : Thou
shalt take away their breath, and
they shall fail, and shall return to
their dust.   Thou shalt send forth

Thy spirit, and they shall be created: and Thou shalt renew the face of the earth (*Ps.* ciii. 24).

Are not two sparrows sold for a farthing? and not one of them shall fall on the ground without your Father. But the very hairs of your head are all numbered. Fear not therefore: better are you than many sparrows (*S. Matt.* x. 30).

Q. Had God any beginning?
A. No: He always was, He is, and He always will be.

I am alpha and omega, the beginning and the end, saith the Lord God, who is, and who was, and who is to come, the Almighty (*Apoc.* i. 8).

But of this one thing be not ignorant, my beloved, that one day with the Lord, is as a thousand years, and a thousand years as one day (2 *S. Peter* iii. 8).

For a thousand years in Thy sight are as yesterday, which is past. And as a watch in the night, as things that are counted nothing, shall their years be (*Ps.* lxxxix. 4).

Before the mountains were made, or the earth and the world was formed: from eternity and to eternity Thou art God (*Ps.* lxxxix. 2).

The number of the days of men at the most are a hundred years: as a drop of water of the sea are they esteemed: and as a pebble of the sand, so are a few years compared to eternity (*Ecclus.* xviii. 8).

Q. Where is God?
A. God is every where.

Whither shall I go from Thy spirit? or whither shall I flee from Thy face? If I ascend into heaven, Thou art there: if I descend into hell, Thou art present. If I take my wings early in the morning, and dwell in the uttermost parts of the sea: even there also shall Thy hand lead me, and Thy right hand shall hold me. And I said: Perhaps darkness shall cover me : and night shall be my light in my pleasures. But darkness shall not be dark to Thee, and night shall be light as the day : the darkness thereof, and the light thereof are alike to Thee (*Ps.* cxxxviii. 7).

For in Him we live and move and are (*Acts* xvii. 28).

Q. Does God know and see all things ?

A. Yes ; God does know and see all things, even our most secret thoughts.

O the depth of the riches of the wisdom and of the knowledge of God! How incomprehensible are His judgments, and how unsearchable His ways! For who hath known the mind of the Lord? or who hath been His counsellor ? (*Rom.* xi. 33.)

But thou when thou shalt pray, enter into thy chamber, and having shut the door, pray to thy Father in secret : and thy Father who seeth in secret will repay thee (*S. Matt.* vi. 6).

Say not : I shall be hidden from God, and who shall remember me from on high ? In such a multitude I shall not be known : for what is my soul in such an immense creation ? (*Ecclus.* xvi. 16.)

Q. Has God any body?

A. No ; God is a pure Spirit.

God is a Spirit, and they that adore Him, must adore Him in spirit and in truth (*S. John* iv. 24).

Q. Are there more Gods than one?

A. No ; there is but one God.

See ye that I alone am, and there is no other God besides Me : I will kill, and I will make to live : I will strike, and I will heal, and there is none that can deliver out of My hand. I will lift My hand to heaven, and I will say : I live for ever. If I shall whet My sword as the lightning, and My hand take hold on judgment : I will render vengeance to My enemies, and repay them that hate Me (*Deut.* xxxii. 39).

For there is no other God but Thou, who hast care of all, that Thou shouldst show that Thou dost not give judgment unjustly (*Wisd.* xii. 13).

Q. Are there more Persons than one in God?

A. Yes; in God there are three Persons; God the Father, God the Son, and God the Holy Ghost.

Q. Are these three Persons then three Gods?

A. No; the Father, the Son, and the Holy Ghost, are all one and the same God.

Q. What is this mystery called?

A. It is called the mystery of the Blessed Trinity.

Q. Is there any kind of likeness of the Blessed Trinity in your soul?

A. Yes; for as in one God there are three Persons, so in my one soul there are three powers.

Q. Which are these three powers?

A. My understanding, my memory, and my will.

For there are three who give testimony in heaven, the Father, the Word, and the Holy Ghost. And these three are One (1 *S. John* v. 7).

THE SECOND ARTICLE.

Q. What is the second article of the Creed?

A. And in Jesus Christ, His only Son, our Lord.

Who being in the form of God, thought it not robbery to be equal with God: but debased Himself, taking the form of a servant, being made in the likeness of men, and

Q. Who is Jesus Christ?

A. He is God the Son, made man for us.

Q. Is Jesus Christ truly God?

A. Yes; He is truly God.

Q. Why is Jesus Christ truly God?

A. Because He has one and the same nature with God the Father.

in habit found as a man (*Phil.* ii. 6).

And the Word was made flesh, and dwelt among us (and we saw His glory, the glory as it were of the only begotten of the Father) full of grace and truth (*S. John* i. 14).

And Jesus being baptized, forthwith came out of the water: and lo! the heavens were opened to him: and he saw the Spirit of God descending as a dove, and coming upon Him. And behold a voice from heaven, saying: This is My beloved Son, in whom I am well pleased (*S. Matt.* iii. 16).

Simon Peter answered and said: Thou art Christ the Son of the living God (*S. Matt.* xvi. 16).

Jesus saith to him: So long a time have I been with you, and have you not known Me? Philip, he that seeth Me, seeth the Father also (*S. John* xiv. 9).

Who being the brightness of His glory, and the figure of His substance, and upholding all things by the word of His power, making purgation of sins, sitteth on the right hand of the Majesty on high (*Heb.* i. 3).

And to the angels indeed He saith: He that maketh His angels spirits, and His ministers a flame of fire. But to the Son: Thy throne, O God, is for ever and ever: a sceptre of justice is the sceptre of Thy kingdom (*Heb.* i. 7.)

For what the law could not do in that it was weak through the flesh: God sending His Son in the likeness of sinful flesh, and of sin, hath condemned sin in the flesh (*Rom.* viii. 3).

Nathanael answered Him, and

said : Rabbi, Thou art the Son of God, Thou art the King of Israel (*S. John* i. 49).

Then rising up, He commanded the winds and the sea, and there came a great calm. But the men wondered, saying : What manner of man is this, for the winds and the sea obey Him? And when He was come on the other side of the water, into the country of the Gerasens, there met Him two that were possessed with devils, coming out of the sepulchres, exceeding fierce, so that none could pass by that way. And behold they cried out, saying : What have we to do with Thee, Jesus, Son of God? art Thou come hither to torment us before the time? (*S. Matt.* viii. 26.)

And I saw heaven opened, and behold a white horse : and He that sat upon him, was called Faithful and True, and with justice doth He judge and fight. And His eyes were as a flame of fire, and on His head were many diadems, and He had a name written, which no man knoweth but Himself. And He was clothed with a garment sprinkled with blood : and His name is called : The Word of God. And the armies that are in heaven followed Him on white horses, clothed in fine linen white and clean. And out of His mouth proceedeth a sharp two-edged sword : that with it He may strike the nations. And He shall rule them with a rod of iron : and He treadeth the wine-press of the fierceness of the wrath of God the Almighy. And He hath on His garment, and on His thigh written : King of Kings and Lord of Lords (*Apoc.* xix. 11).

Q. Was Jesus Christ always God?

In the beginning was the Word, and the Word was with God, and

A. Yes ; He was always God : born of the Father from all eternity.

the Word was God. The same was in the beginning with God. All things were made by Him : and without Him was made nothing that was made (*S. John* i. 1).

The Jews therefore said to Him : Thou art not yet fifty years old, and hast Thou seen Abraham? Jesus said to them : Amen, amen, I say to you, before Abraham was made, I am (*S. John* viii. 57).

Q. Which Person of the Blessed Trinity is Jesus Christ ?
A. He is the second Person of the Blessed Trinity.

Q. Is Jesus Christ truly man ?
A. Yes ; He is truly man.

For we have not a high priest who cannot have compassion on our infirmities : but one tempted in all things like as we are, without sin (*Heb.* iv. 15).

And when He had fasted forty days and forty nights, afterwards he was hungry (*S. Matt.* iv. 2).

But they being troubled and frighted, supposed that they saw a spirit. And He said to them : Why are you troubled, and why do thoughts arise in your hearts? See My hands and feet, that it is I Myself; handle, and see : for a spirit hath not flesh and bones, as you see Me to have. And when He had said this, He showed them His hands and feet. But while they yet believed not, and wondered for joy, He said : Have you here any thing to eat? And they offered Him a piece of a broiled fish and a honey-comb (*S. Luke* xxiv. 37).

Q. Why is He truly man ?

And this shall be a sign unto you. You shall find the infant wrapped in

A. Because He has the nature of man, having a body and soul like ours.

Q. Was Jesus Christ always man?
A. No; He has been man only from the time of His Incarnation.

Q. What do you mean by His Incarnation?
A. I mean His taking to Himself our human nature.

Q. How many natures, then, are there in Jesus Christ?
A. There are two; the nature of God, and the nature of man.

Q. Are there two Persons also in Jesus Christ?
A. No; in Jesus Christ there is only one Person, which is the Person of God the Son.

Q. Why was God the Son made man?

swaddling clothes, and laid in a manger (*S. Luke* ii. 12).

Then He saith to them : My soul is sorrowful even unto death : stay you here, and watch with Me (*S. Matt.* xxvi. 38).

But when the fulness of the time was come, God sent His Son, made of a woman, made under the law : that He might redeem them who were under the law; that we might receive the adoption of sons (*Gal.* iv. 4).

Behold thou shalt conceive in thy womb, and shalt bring forth a son : and thou shalt call His name Jesus. He shall be great, and shall be called the Son of the Most High, and the Lord God shall give unto Him the throne of David His father; and He shall reign in the house of Jacob for ever, and of His kingdom there shall be no end (*S. Luke* i. 31).

And about the ninth hour Jesus cried with a loud voice, saying : Eli, Eli, lamma sabacthani? that is, My God, my God, why hast Thou forsaken me? (*S. Matt.* xxvii. 46.)

I and the Father are one. The Jews then took up stones to stone Him. Jesus answered them : Many good works I have shewed you from My Father; for which of those works do you stone Me? The Jews answered Him : For a good work we stone Thee not, but for blasphemy; and because that Thou being a man, makest Thyself God (*S. John* x. 30).

Who His ownself bore our sins in His body upon the tree : that we

c

A. To redeem us from sin and hell.

being dead to sins, should live to justice : by whose stripes you were healed (1 *S. Peter* ii. 24).

But when the fulness of the time was come, God sent His Son, made of a woman, made under the law : that He might redeem them who were under the law; that we might receive the adoption of sons (*Gal.* iv. 4).

Q. What means the holy name Jesus ?
A. Saviour (*Matt.* i. 21).

And she shall bring forth a Son : and thou shalt call His name Jesus. For He shall save His people from their sins (*S. Matt.* i. 21).

For which cause God also hath exalted Him, and hath given Him a name which is above all names : that in the name of Jesus every knee should bow, of those that are in heaven, on earth, and under the earth : and that every tongue should confess that the Lord Jesus Christ is in the glory of God the Father (*Phil.* ii. 9).

But I will rejoice in the Lord : and I will joy in God my Jesus (*Hab.* iii. 18).

Be it known to you all, and to all the people of Israel, that by the name of our Lord Jesus Christ of Nazareth, whom you crucified, whom God hath raised from the dead, even by Him this man standeth here before you whole. This is the stone which was rejected by you the builders; which is become the head of the corner. Neither is their salvation in any other. For there is no other name under heaven given to men, whereby we must be saved (*Acts* iv. 10).

Q. What means the name Christ ?
A. Anointed.

Seventy weeks are shortened upon Thy people, and upon Thy holy city, that transgression may be finished, and sin may have an end, and iniquity may be abolished ; and ever-lasting justice may be brought ; and vision and prophecy may be fulfilled ; and the Saint of Saints may be anointed (*Dan.* ix. 24).

The Spirit of the Lord is upon Me, because the Lord hath anointed Me : He hath sent Me to preach to the meek, to heal the contrite of heart, and to preach a release to the captives, and deliverance to them that are shut up (*Isa.* lxi. 1).

THE THIRD ARTICLE.

Q. What is the third article of the Creed ?

A. Who was conceived by the Holy Ghost, born of the Virgin Mary.

The Holy Ghost shall come upon thee, and the power of the most High shall overshadow thee. And therefore also the Holy which shall be born of thee shall be called the Son of God (*S. Luke* i. 35).

Prophecies of the Incarnation.

Q. What means this article?

A. It means that God the Son took flesh, and was made man by the power of the Holy Ghost in the womb of the Blessed Virgin Mary, without having any man for his Father.

I will put enmities between thee and the woman, and thy seed and her seed : she shall crush thy head, and thou shalt lie in wait for her heel (*Gen.* iii. 15).

And in thy seed shall all the nations of the earth be blessed, because thou hast obeyed My voice (*Gen.* xxii. 18).

And I will multiply thy seed like the stars of heaven : and I will give to thy posterity all these countries : and in thy seed shall all the nations of the earth be blessed (*Gen.* xxvi. 4).

The sceptre shall not be taken away from Juda, nor a ruler from his thigh, till He come that is to be sent, and He shall be the expectation of nations (*Gen.* xlix. 10).

The blessings of thy father are strengthened with the blessings of his fathers : until the desire of the everlasting hills should come (*Gen.* xlix. 26).

A star shall rise out of Jacob and a sceptre shall spring up from Israel (*Num.* xxiv. 17).

And there shall come forth a rod out of the root of Jesse, and a flower shall rise up out of his root. And the Spirit of the Lord shall rest upon him : the spirit of wisdom, and of understanding, the spirit of counsel, and of fortitude, the spirit of knowledge, and of godliness (*Isa.* xi. 1).

Therefore the Lord himself shall give you a sign. Behold a virgin shall conceive, and bear a Son, and His name shall be called Emmanuel (*Isa.* vii. 14).

For a child is born to us, and a Son is given to us, and the government is upon His shoulder : and His name shall be called, Wonderful, Counsellor, God, the Mighty, the Father of the world to come, the Prince of Peace (*Isa.* ix. 6).

Know thou therefore, and take notice : that from the going forth of the word, to build up Jerusalem again, unto Christ the Prince, there shall be seven weeks, and sixty-two weeks : and the street shall be built again, and the walls in straitness of times. And after sixty-two weeks Christ shall be slain : and the people that shall deny Him shall not be His. And a people with their leader that shall come, shall destroy the city and the sanctuary : and the end thereof shall be waste, and after the end of the war the appointed desolation. And He shall confirm the covenant with many, in one week : and in the half of the week the victim and the sacrifice shall fail : and there shall be in the temple the abomination of desolation : and the desolation shall continue even to the consummation, and to the end (*Dan.* ix. 25).

Behold I send My Angel, and he shall prepare the way before My face. And presently the Lord, whom you seek, and the Angel of the testament, whom you desire, shall come to His temple. Behold He cometh, saith the Lord of Hosts (*Mal.* iii. 1).

And thou, Bethlehem Ephrata, art a little one among the thousands of Juda : out of thee shall He come forth unto Me that is to be the ruler in Israel, and His going forth is from the beginning, from the days of eternity (*Micheas* v. 2).

Q. Where was our Saviour born?
A. In a stable at Bethlehem.

And it came to pass, after the angels departed from them into heaven, the shepherds said one to another: Let us go over to Bethlehem, and let us see this word that is come to pass, which the Lord hath showed to us. And they came with haste : and they found Mary and Joseph, and the Infant lying in a manger (*S. Luke* ii. 15).

Q. Upon what day was He born?
A. Upon Christmas-day.

And the angel said to them : Fear not ; for behold I bring you good tidings of great joy, that shall be to all the people : for this day is born to you a Saviour, who is Christ the Lord, in the city of David (*S. Luke* ii. 10).

Prophecies of the Passion-Words of our Lord.

THE FOURTH ARTICLE.

Q. What is the fourth article of the Creed?
A. Suffered under Pontius Pilate, was crucified, dead, and buried.

Behold we go up to Jerusalem, and the Son of Man shall be betrayed to the chief priests and the scribes, and they shall condemn Him to death, and shall deliver Him to the gentiles to be mocked, and scourged, and crucified, and the third day he shall rise again (*S. Matt.* xx. 18).

The Son of Man indeed goeth, as

is written of Him : but woe to that man, by whom the Son of Man shall be betrayed : it were better for him, if that man had not been born (*S. Matt.* xxvi. 24).

For she in pouring this ointment upon My body, hath done it for My burial (*S. Matt.* xxvi. 12).

And I, if I be lifted up from the earth, will draw all things to Myself. (Now this He said, signifying what death He should die) (*S. John* xii. 32).

Other Prophecies.

But He was wounded for our iniquities, He was bruised for our sins : the chastisement of our peace was upon Him, and by His bruises we are healed (*Isa.* liii. 5).

He was offered because it was His own will, and He opened not His mouth : He shall be led as a sheep to the slaughter, and shall be dumb as a lamb before His shearer, and He shall not open His mouth (*Isa.* liii. 7).

They have dug My hands and feet : they have numbered all My bones (*Ps.* xxi. 17).

For I am ready for scourges : and My sorrow is continually before Me (*Ps.* xxxvii. 18).

And they gave Me gall for My food, and in My thirst they gave Me vinegar to drink (*Ps.* lxviii. 22).

Q. What were the chief sufferings of Christ?

A. His sweat of blood, His scourging at the Pillar, His crowning with thorns, and the carrying of His Cross.

And taking with Him Peter and the two sons of Zebedee, He began to grow sorrowful and to be sad. Then He saith to them : My soul is sorrowful even unto death : stay you here, and watch with Me. And going a little further, He fell upon His face, praying, and saying : My Father, if it be possible, let this chalice pass from me. Nevertheless not as I will, but as Thou wilt (*S. Matt.* xxvi. 37).

And there appeared to Him an Angel from heaven strengthening Him. And being in an agony, He prayed the longer. And His sweat became as drops of blood trickling down upon the ground (*S. Luke* xxii. 43).

Then he released to them Barabbas, and having scourged Jesus, delivered Him unto them to be crucified. Then the soldiers of the governor taking Jesus into the hall, gathered together unto Him the whole band: and stripping Him, they put a scarlet cloak about Him. And platting a crown of thorns, they put it upon His head, and a reed in His right hand. And bowing the knee before Him, they mocked Him, saying: Hail, King of the Jews (*S. Matt.* xxvii. 26).

And bearing His own cross He went forth to that place which is called Calvary, but in Hebrew Golgotha (*S. John* xix. 17).

Q. What else did He suffer?

A. He was nailed to the Cross, and died upon it between two thieves.

And they put over His head His cause written: This is Jesus the King of the Jews. Then were crucified with Him two thieves: one on the right hand, and one on the left (*S. Matt.* xxvii. 37).

And Jesus again crying with a loud voice, yielded up the ghost. And behold the veil of the temple was rent in two from the top even to the bottom, and the earth quaked, and the rocks were rent. And the graves were opened: and many bodies of the saints that had slept, arose (*S. Matt.* xxvii. 50).

Q. Why did He suffer?

A. For our sins.

For the wickedness of My people have I struck Him (*Isa.* liii. 8).

Now once at the end of ages, He

hath appeared for the destruction of sin, by the sacrifice of Himself (*Heb.* ix. 26).

So also Christ was offered once to exhaust the sins of many (*Heb.*ix. 28).

Q. Upon what day did He suffer?

A. On Good Friday.

Then the Jews (because it was the parasceve) that the bodies might not remain upon the cross on the Sabbath-day (for that was a great Sabbath-day), besought Pilate that their legs might be broken, and that they might be taken away (*S. John* xix. 31).

Q. Where did he suffer?

A. On Mount Calvary.

And they came to the place that is called Golgotha, which is the place of Calvary (*S. Matt.* xxvii. 33).

Q. Why do we make the sign of the Cross[1]?

A. To put us in mind of the Blessed Trinity; and that God the Son died for us upon the Cross.

And then shall appear the sign of the Son of Man in heaven (*S. Matt.* xxiv. 30).

Hurt not the earth, nor the sea, nor the trees, till we sign the servants of our God in their foreheads (*Apoc.* vii. 3).

But God forbid that I should glory, save in the cross of our Lord Jesus Christ; by whom the world is crucified to me, and I to the world (*Gal.* vi. 14).

Q. What puts us in mind of the Blessed Trinity, when we make the sign of the Cross?

A. The words: In the name of the Father, and of the Son, and of the Holy Ghost.

Q. What puts us in mind that Christ suffered for us on the Cross?

---

[1] See note A, Testimony of the Fathers to the ancient use of the Sign of the Cross.

A. The very form of the Cross which we make on ourselves.

THE FIFTH ARTICLE.

Q. What is the fifth article of the Creed?

A. He descended into hell; the third day He rose again from the dead.

In which also coming He preached to those spirits that were in prison (1 *S. Pet.* iii. 19).

Q. What means, He descended into hell?

A. It means, that as soon as Christ was dead, His soul went down into that part of hell called Limbo.

Wherefore He saith: Ascending on high He led captivity captive; He gave gifts to men. Now that He ascended, what is it, but because He also descended first into the lower parts of the earth? (*Eph.* iv. 8.)

Q. What do you mean by Limbo?

A. I mean a place of rest, where the souls of the just who died before Christ were detained.

And it came to pass that the beggar died, and was carried by the Angels into Abraham's bosom (*S. Luke* xvi. 22).

Q. Why were they detained there?

A. Because none could go up to Heaven before our Saviour.

I will break in pieces the gates of brass, and will burst the bars of iron (*Isa.* xlv. 2).

And He is the head of the body, the Church, who is the beginning, the first-born from the dead (*Col.* i. 18).

Prophecy of the Resurrection.

Q. What means, the third day He rose again from the dead?

A. It means, that after Christ had been dead and buried part of three days, He raised His Blessed Body to life again on the third day.

For as Jonas was in the whale's belly three days and three nights: so shall the Son of Man be in the heart of the earth three days and three nights (*S. Matt.* xii. 40).

Jesus answered, and said to them: Destroy this temple, and in three days I will raise it up. The Jews then said: Six and forty years was this temple in building, and wilt thou raise it up in three days? But He spoke of the temple of His body.

When therefore He was risen again from the dead, His disciples remembered that He had said this, and they believed the scripture, and the word that Jesus had said (*S. John* ii. 19).

History of the Resurrection.

And in the end of the Sabbath when it began to dawn towards the first day of the week came Mary Magdalene and the other Mary to see the sepulchre. And behold there was a great earthquake. For an Angel of the Lord descended from heaven : and coming, rolled back the stone, and sat upon it : and his countenance was as lightning, and his raiment as snow. And for fear of him, the guards were struck with terror, and became as dead men. And the Angel answering, said to the women : Fear not you : for I know that you seek Jesus who was crucified. He is not here, for He is risen, as He said. Come, and see the place where the Lord was laid (*S. Matt.* xxviii. 1).

They say to her : Woman, why weepest thou ? She saith to them : Because they have taken away my Lord : and I know not where they have laid Him. When she had thus said, she turned herself back, and saw Jesus standing ; and she knew not that it was Jesus (*S. John* xx. 13).

But when the morning was come, Jesus stood on the shore : yet the disciples knew not that it was Jesus (*S. John* xxi. 4).

And it came to pass, that while they talked and reasoned with themselves, Jesus himself also drawing near went with them. But their eyes were held that they should not know Him (*S. Luke* xxiv. 15).

Then He said to them : O foolish,

and slow of heart to believe in all things which the prophets have spoken. Ought not Christ to have suffered these things, and so to enter into His glory? (*S. Luke* xxiv. 25.)

Importance of Christ's Resurrection.

And if Christ be not risen again, then is our preaching vain, and your faith is also vain (1 *Cor.* xv. 14).

But now Christ is risen from the dead, the first-fruits of them that sleep (1 *Cor.* xv. 20).

Q. On what day did Christ rise again from the dead?

A. On Easter Sunday.

And when the sabbath was past, Mary Magdalen and Mary the mother of James and Salome bought sweet spices, that coming they might anoint Jesus. And very early in the morning the first day of the week, they came to the sepulchre, the sun being now risen. And they said one to another: Who shall roll us back the stone from the door of the sepulchre? And looking, they saw the stone rolled back. For it was very great. And entering into the sepulchre, they saw a young man sitting on the right side, clothed with a white robe: and they were astonished. Who saith to them: Be not affrighted; ye seek Jesus of Nazareth, who was crucified: He is risen, He is not here, behold the place where they laid Him (*S. Mark* xvi. 1).

THE SIXTH ARTICLE.

Q. What is the sixth article of the Creed?

A. He ascended into Heaven, sitteth at the right hand of God the Father Almighty.

And when He had said these things, while they looked on, He was raised up: and a cloud received Him out of their sight (*Acts* i. 9).

And the Lord Jesus, after He had spoken to them, was taken up into Heaven, and sitteth on the right hand of God (*S. Mark* xvi. 19).

Lift up your gates, O ye princes,

and be ye lifted up, O eternal gates : and the King of Glory shall enter in. Who is this King of Glory? the Lord who is strong and mighty : the Lord mighty in battle. Lift up your gates, O ye princes, and be ye lifted up, O eternal gates : and the King of Glory shall enter in. Who is this King of Glory? the Lord of hosts, He is the King of Glory (*Ps.* xxiii. 7).

Q. What means, sitteth at the right hand of God the Father Almighty?

A. Not that God the Father has hands, for He is a pure spirit : but that Christ, as man, holds the next place to God in Heaven.

For He must reign, until He hath put all enemies under His feet (1 *Cor.* xv. 25).

Therefore, if you be risen with Christ, seek the things that are above, where Christ is sitting at the right hand of God : mind the things that are above, not the things that are upon the earth (*Col.* iii. 1).

Q. Why do you say as man?

A. Because as God He is equal to the Father in all things.

Who being in the form of God, thought it not robbery, to be equa with God (*Phil.* ii. 6).

Q. When did our Saviour go up to Heaven?

A. On Ascension-day; forty days after He had risen again.

To whom also He shewed Himself alive after His passion, by many proofs, for forty days appearing to them, and speaking of the kingdom of God (*Acts* i. 3).

But there are also many other things which Jesus did; which, if they were written every one, the world itself, I think, would not be able to contain the books that should be written (*S. John* xxi. 25).

THE SEVENTH ARTICLE.

Q. What is the seventh article of the Creed?

A. From thence He shall come to judge the living and the dead.

Ye men of Galilee, why stand you looking up to heaven? This Jesus who is taken up from you into heaven, shall so come as you have seen Him going into heaven (*Acts* i. 11).

Q. Will Christ ever come again?

A. Yes; He will come down from Heaven at the last day, to judge all men.

For as lightning cometh out of the east, and appeareth even into the west : so also shall the coming of the Son of Man be (*S. Matt.* xxiv. 27).

And all nations shall be gathered together before Him, and He shall separate them one from another, as the shepherd separateth the sheep from the goats (*S. Matt.* xxv. 32).

Behold, He cometh with the clouds, and every eye shall see Him, and they also that pierced Him. And all the tribes of the earth shall bewail themselves because of Him. Even so. Amen (*Apoc.* i. 7).

Q. What are the things He will judge?

A. All our thoughts, words, and works.

But I say unto you, that every idle word that men shall speak, they shall render an account for it in the day of judgment (*S. Matt.* xii. 36).

And I saw the dead, great and small, standing in the presence of the throne, and the books were opened : and another book was opened, which is the book of life : and the dead were judged by those things which were written in the books, according to their works (*Apoc.* xx. 12).

Q. What will He say to the wicked?

A. "Depart from Me, you cursed, into everlasting fire."

Many will say to Me in that day : Lord, Lord, have we not prophesied in Thy name, and cast out devils in Thy name, and done many miracles in Thy name? And then will I profess unto them, I never knew you : depart from Me, you that work iniquity (*S. Matt.* vii. 22).

And he cried, and said : Father Abraham, have mercy on me, and send Lazarus that he may dip the tip of his finger in water, to cool my tongue, for I am tormented in this flame (*S. Luke* xvi. 24).

And whosoever was not found written in the book of life, was cast into the pool of fire (*Apoc.* xx. 15).

But the fearful, and unbelieving, and the abominable, and murderers, and whoremongers, and sorcerers, and idolaters, and all liars, they shall have their portion in the pool burning with fire and brimstone, which is the second death (*Apoc.* xxi. 8).

And the smoke of their torments shall ascend up for ever and ever : neither have they rest day nor night, who have adored the beast, and his image, and whosoever receiveth the character of his name (*Apoc.* xiv. 11).

And they shall go out, and see the carcasses of the men that have transgressed against Me : their worm shall not die, and their fire shall not be quenched : and they shall be a loathsome sight to all flesh (*Isa.* lxvi. 24).

For Topheth is prepared from yesterday, prepared by the king, deep, and wide. The nourishments thereof are fire and much wood : the breath of the Lord as a torrent of brimstone kindling it (*Isa.* xxx. 33).

Q. What will He say to the just?

A. " Come, ye blessed of My Father, possess you the kingdom which is prepared for you " (*Matt.* xxv. 34).

And every one that hath left house, or brethren, or sisters, or father, or mother, or wife, or children, or lands for My name's sake : shall receive an hundred fold, and shall possess life everlasting (*S. Matt.* xix. 29).

But, as it is written : That eye hath not seen, nor ear heard, neither hath it entered into the heart of man, what things God hath prepared for them that love Him (1 *Cor.* ii. 9).

And God shall wipe away all tears from their eyes : and death shall be no more, nor mourning, nor crying, nor sorrow shall be any more, for the former things are passed away (*Apoc.* xxi. 4).

And He took me up in spirit to a great and high mountain : and He shewed me the holy city Jerusalem coming down out of heaven from God, having the glory of God, and the light thereof was like to a precious stone, as to the jasper-stone, even as crystal (*Apoc.* xxi. 10).

And the city hath no need of the sun, nor of the moon to shine in it. For the glory of God hath enlightened it, and the Lamb is the lamp thereof (*Apoc.* xxi. 23).

Q. Will not every man be judged at his death, as well as at the last day?

A. Yes: "It is appointed unto men once to die, and after this, the judgment " (*Heb.* ix. 27).

THE EIGHTH ARTICLE.

Q. What is the eighth article of the Creed?

A. I believe in the Holy Ghost.

Going therefore teach ye all nations : baptizing them in the name of the Father, and of the Son, and of the Holy Ghost (*S. Matt.* xxviii. 19).

Q. Who is the Holy Ghost?

A. He is the third Person of the Blessed Trinity.

The grace of our Lord Jesus Christ, and the charity of God, and the communication of the Holy Ghost be with you all. Amen (*2 Cor.* xiii. 13).

And the Holy Ghost descended in a bodily shape as a dove upon Him : and a voice came from heaven : Thou art My beloved Son, in Thee I am well pleased (*S. Luke* iii. 22).

And He said to them : Have you received the Holy Ghost since ye believed? But they said to Him : We have not so much as heard whether there be a Holy Ghost. And He said : In what then were you baptized? Who said : In John's baptism. Then Paul said, John baptized the people with the baptism of penance, saying : That they should believe in Him who was to come after him, that is to say, in Jesus. Having heard these things they were baptized in the name of the Lord Jesus. And when Paul had imposed his hands on them, the Holy Ghost came upon them, and they spoke with tongues and prophesied (*Acts* xix. 2).

Q. From whom does He proceed?

A. From the Father and the Son.

But when the Paraclete cometh, whom I will send you from the Father, the Spirit of truth, who proceedeth from the Father, He shall give testimony of Me (*S. John* xv. 26).

But when He the Spirit of truth, is come, He will teach you all truth. For He shall not speak of Himself : but what things soever He shall hear, He shall speak, and the things that are to come He shall shew you. He shall glorify Me ; because He shall receive of Mine, and shall shew it to you (*S. John* xvi. 13).

And because you are sons, God hath sent the Spirit of His Son into your hearts, crying : Abba, Father (*Gal.* iv. 6).

Q. Is He equal to them?

A. Yes; He is the same Lord and God as they are.

And I will ask the Father, and He shall give you another Paraclete, that He may abide with you for ever (*S. John* xiv. 16).

But Peter said : Ananias, why hath Satan tempted thy heart, that thou shouldst lie to the Holy Ghost, and by fraud keep part of the price of the land ? Whilst it remained, did it not remain to thee ? and after it was sold, was it not in thy power? Why hast thou conceived this thing in thy heart? Thou hast not lied to men, but to God (*Acts* v. 3).

Q. When did the Holy Ghost come down

And when the days of the pentecost were accomplished, they were on the Apostles in fiery tongues?

A. On Whit-Sunday.

all together in one place : and suddenly there came a sound from heaven, as of a mighty wind coming, and it filled the whole house where they were sitting. And there appeared to them parted tongues as it were of fire, and it sat upon every one of them : and they were all filled with the Holy Ghost, and they began to speak with divers tongues, according as the Holy Ghost gave them to speak (*Acts* ii. 1).

Q. Why did He come down upon them?

A. To enable them to preach the Gospel, and to plant the Church.

But you shall receive the power of the Holy Ghost coming upon you, and you shall be witnesses unto Me in Jerusalem, and in all Judea, and Samaria, and even to the uttermost part of the earth (*Acts* i. 8).

But the Paraclete, the Holy Ghost, whom the Father will send in My name, He will teach you all things, and bring all things to your mind, whatsoever I shall have said to you (*S. John* xiv. 26).

For it is not you that speak, but the Spirit of your Father that speaketh in you (*S. Matt.* x. 20).

But all these things one and the same Spirit worketh, dividing to every one according as He will (1 *Cor.* xii. 11).

Christ the Head of the whole Church, comprising Church Militant, Church Suffering, and Church Glorious.

THE NINTH ARTICLE.

Q. What is the ninth article of the Creed?

A. The Holy Catholic Church ; the Communion of Saints.

Q. What is the Catholic Church?

A. The union of all the faithful under one head.

But you are come to Mount Sion, and to the city of the living God, the Heavenly Jerusalem, and to the company of many thousands of Angels, and to the Church of the first-born, who are written in the Heavens, and to God the Judge of all, and to the spirits of the just made perfect, and to Jesus the Mediator of the New Testament, and to the sprinkling of blood which

D

Q. Who is that head?
A. Christ Jesus our Lord.

speaketh better than that of Abel (*Heb.* xii. 22).

And He hath subjected all things under His feet: and hath made Him head over all the Church, which is His body (*Eph.* i. 22).

Giving thanks to God the Father, who hath made us worthy to be partakers of the lot of the Saints in light, who hath delivered us from the power of darkness, and hath translated us into the Kingdom of the Son of His love (*Col.* i. 12).

And He is the head of the body, the Church, who is the beginning, the first-born from the dead : that in all things He may hold the primacy (*Col.* i. 18).

Prophecies of the Church.

And in the last days the mountain of the House of the Lord shall be prepared on the top of mountains, and it shall be exalted above the hills, and all nations shall flow unto it. And many people shall go, and say : Come and let us go up to the mountain of the Lord, and to the house of the God of Jacob, and He will teach us His ways, and we will walk in His paths: for the law shall come forth from Sion, and the word of the Lord from Jerusalem (*Isa.* ii. 2).

Thus thou sawest, till a stone was cut out of a mountain without hands : and it struck the statue upon the feet thereof that were of iron and of clay, and broke them in pieces (*Dan.* ii. 34).

But in the days of those kingdoms the God of Heaven will set up a kingdom that shall never be destroyed, and His kingdom shall not be delivered up to another people, and it shall break in pieces, and shall consume all these kingdoms, and itself shall stand for ever (*Dan.* ii. 44).

Q. Has not the Church a visible head on earth?

A. Yes; the Bishop of Rome, who is the Vicar of Christ.

Q. Why is the Bishop of Rome the head of the Church?

A. Because he is the successor of St. Peter, whom Christ appointed to be the head of the Church.

Q. How do you prove that Christ appointed St. Peter to be the head of the Church?

A. Because He said to him: "Thou art Peter, and upon this rock I will build My Church, and the gates of hell shall not prevail against it; and to thee will I give the keys of the kingdom of Heaven" (*Matt.* xvi. 18, 19).

Q. What is the Bishop of Rome called?

A. He is called the Pope, which word signifies Father.

Q. Is then the Pope our spiritual Father?

A. Yes; he is the spiritual Father of all the faithful.

Supremacy of St. Peter[1].

He saith unto them, But whom say ye that I am? And Simon Peter answered and said, Thou art the Christ, the Son of the living God. And Jesus answered and said unto him, Blessed art thou, Simon Bar-jona : for flesh and blood hath not revealed it unto thee, but My Father who is in Heaven. And I say also unto thee, That thou art Peter, and upon this rock I will build My Church ; and the gates of hell shall not prevail against it. And I will give unto thee the keys of the King-dom of Heaven; and whatsoever thou shalt bind on earth shall be bound in Heaven, and whatsoever thou shalt loose on earth shall be loosed in Heaven (*S. Matt.* xvi. 15).

When therefore they had dined, Jesus saith to Simon Peter : Simon son of John, lovest thou Me more than these? He saith to Him : Yea, Lord, Thou knowest that I love Thee. He saith to him : Feed My lambs. He saith to him again : Simon son of John, lovest thou Me ? He saith to Him : Yea, Lord, Thou knowest that I love Thee. He saith to him : Feed My lambs. He said to him, the third time : Simon son of John, lovest thou Me ? Peter was grieved, because He said to him the third time, lovest thou Me ? And he said to Him : Lord, Thou know-est all things : Thou knowest that I love Thee. He said to him : Feed My sheep (*S. John* xxi. 15).

And the Lord said : Simon, Si-mon, behold Satan hath desired to have you, that he may sift you as wheat. But I have prayed for thee that thy faith fail not : and thou

[1] See note B, on the Supremacy of the Pope in the Early Church.

being once converted confirm thy brethren (*S. Luke* xxii. 31).

The Church Visible.

Q. Has the Church of Christ any marks by which you may know her?

A. Yes; she has these four marks : she is One —she is Holy—she is Catholic—she is Apostolic.

And other sheep I have, that are not of this fold : them also I must bring, and they shall hear My voice, and there shall be one fold and one Shepherd (*S. John* x. 16).

Then shall the Kingdom of Heaven be like to ten virgins, who taking their lamps went out to meet the bridegroom and the bride. And five of them were foolish, and five wise. But the five foolish, having taken their lamps, did not take oil with them : But the wise took oil in their vessels with the lamps (*S. Matt.* xxv. 1).

Again the Kingdom of Heaven is like to a net cast into the sea, and gathering together of all kind of fishes (*S. Matt.* xiii. 47).

One body and one Spirit : as you are called in one hope of your calling (*Eph.* iv. 4).

The Church an organized Body—not a mere collection of individuals.

And He gave some apostles, and some prophets, and other some evangelists, and other some pastors and doctors. For the perfecting of the Saints, for the work of the ministry, for the edifying of the body of Christ (*Eph.* iv. 11).

Now you are the body of Christ, and members of member. And God indeed hath set some in the Church, first apostles, secondly, prophets, thirdly doctors, after that miracles, then the graces of healings, helps, governments, kinds of tongues, interpretations of speeches (1 *Cor.* xii. 27).

Take heed to yourselves, and to the whole flock, wherein the Holy

Ghost hath placed you bishops, to rule the Church of God, which He hath purchased with His own blood. I know that after my departure ravening wolves will enter in among you, not sparing the flock. And of your own selves shall arise men speaking perverse things, to draw away disciples after them. Therefore watch, keeping in memory, that for three years I ceased not with tears to admonish every one of you night and day (*Acts* xx. 28).

Feed the flock of God which is among you, taking care of it not by constraint, but willingly according to God : not for filthy lucre's sake, but voluntarily : Neither as lording it over the clergy, but being made a pattern of the flock from the heart (1 *S. Pet.* v. 2).

But if a man know not how to rule his own house, how shall he take care of the Church of God ? (1 *Tim.* iii. 5.)

Let no man despise thy youth : but be thou an example of the faithful, in word, in conversation, in charity, in faith, in chastity. Till I come, attend unto reading, to exhortation, and to doctrine. Neglect not the grace that is in thee, which was given thee by prophecy, with imposition of the hands of the priesthood (1 *Tim.* iv. 12).

Obey your prelates, and be subject to them. For they watch as being to render an account of your souls (*Heb.* xiii. 17).

We are of God. He that knoweth God, heareth us. He that is not of God, heareth us not. By this we know the spirit of truth, and the spirit of error (1 *S. John* iv. 6).

And One, Holy, Catholic, and Apostolic Church.—Nicene Creed.

Q. How is the Church One?

A. Because all her members agree in one faith ; have all the same sacraments and sacrifice; and are all under one head.

Holy Father, keep them in Thy name, whom Thou hast given Me : that they may be one, as We also are (*S. John* xvii. 11).

Careful to keep the unity of the Spirit in the bond of peace. One body and one Spirit : as you are called in one hope of your calling. One Lord, one faith, one baptism. One God and Father of all, who is above all, and through all, and in us all (*Eph.* iv. 3).

For we, being many, are one bread, one body, all that partake of one bread (1 *Cor.* x. 17).

For as the body is one, and hath many members ; and all the members of the body, whereas they are many, yet are one body : so also is Christ. For in one Spirit were we all baptized into one body, whether Jews, or gentiles, whether bond or free : and in one Spirit we have all been made to drink. For the body also is not one member, but many (1 *Cor.* xii. 12).

For as in one body we have many members, but all the members have not the same office : so we being many, are one body in Christ, and every one members one of another. And having different gifts, according to the grace that is given us (*Rom.* xii. 4).

Q. How is the Church Holy?

A. Because she teaches a holy doctrine, offers to all the means of holiness, and is distinguished by the eminent holiness of so many thousands of her children.

As He chose us in Him before the foundation of the world, that we should be holy and unspotted in His sight in charity (*Eph.* i. 4).

That He might present it to Himself a glorious church, not having spot or wrinkle, or any such thing, but that it should be holy and without blemish (*Eph.* v. 27).

But you are a chosen generation, a kingly priesthood, a holy nation, a purchased people : that you may declare His virtues, who hath called you out of darkness into His marvellous light (1 *S. Pet.* ii. 9).

Holiness becometh Thy house, O Lord, unto length of days (*Ps.* xcii. 5).

Q. What means the word Catholic ?

A. The word Catholic means Universal.

Q. How is the Church Catholic or Universal ?

A. Because she subsists in all ages, teaches all nations, and maintains all truths.

And He said to them : Go ye into the whole world and preach the gospel to every creature (*S. Mark* xvi. 15).

For there is no distinction of the Jew and the Greek : for the same is Lord over all, rich unto all that call upon Him (*Rom.* x. 12).

Their sound hath gone forth into all the earth, and their words unto the ends of the whole world (*Rom.* x. 18).

And Peter opening his mouth, said : In very deed I perceive that God is not a respecter of persons. But in every nation, he that feareth Him, and worketh justice, is acceptable to Him (*Acts* x. 34).

Arise, be enlightened, O Jerusalem : for thy light is come, and the glory of the Lord is risen upon thee. For behold darkness shall cover the earth, and a mist the people : but the Lord shall arise upon thee, and His glory shall be seen upon thee. And the gentiles shall walk in thy light, and kings in the brightness of thy rising. Lift up thy eyes round about, and see: all these are gathered together, they are come to thee : thy sons shall come from afar, and thy daughters shall rise up at thy side. Then shalt thou see, and abound, and thy heart shall wonder and be enlarged, when the multitude of the sea shall be converted to thee, the strength of the gentiles shall come to thee (*Isa.* lx. 1).

After this, I saw a great multitude, which no man could number, of all nations, and tribes, and peoples, and tongues : standing before the throne, and in sight of the Lamb, clothed with white robes, and palms in their hands (*Apoc.* vii. 9).

Q. How is the Church Apostolic ?

A. Because in her pastors she comes down by a continual succession from the Apostles of Christ ; and has her doctrine, her orders, and her mission from them.

He said therefore to them again : Peace be to you. As the Father hath sent Me, I also send you (*S. John* xx. 21).

And He saith to them : Come ye after Me, and I will make you to be fishers of men (*S. Matt.* iv. 19).

How then shall they call on Him, in whom they have not believed ? Or how shall they believe Him, of whom they have not heard ? And how shall they hear, without a preacher ? And how shall they preach unless they be sent, as it is written : How beautiful are the feet of them that preach the gospel of peace, of them that bring glad tidings of good things! (*Rom.* x. 15.)

And they were persevering in the doctrine of the apostles, and in the communication of the breaking of bread, and in prayers (*Acts* ii. 42).

Q. Can the Church err in what she teaches ?

A. No ; she cannot err in faith or morals for she is our infallible guide in both.

Q. What proof have you of this ?

A. Christ has promised that the gates of hell shall not prevail against His Church ; that the Holy Ghost shall teach her all truth, and that He Himself will abide with her for ever.

And Jesus coming spoke to them, saying : All power is given to Me in Heaven and in earth. Going therefore teach ye all nations : baptizing them in the name of the Father, and of the Son, and of the Holy Ghost, teaching them to observe all things whatsoever I have commanded you : and behold I am with you all days, even to the consummation of the world (*S. Matt.* xxviii. 18).

And I say to thee : That thou art Peter ; and upon this rock I will build My church, and the gates of hell shall not prevail against it (*S. Matt.* xvi. 18).

But into whatsoever city you enter, and they receive you not, going forth into the streets thereof, say : Even the very dust of your city that cleaveth to us we wipe off against you. You know this that the kingdom of God is at hand. I say to you, it shall be more tolerable at that day for Sodom, than for that city (*S. Luke* x. 10).

He that heareth you, heareth Me : and he that despiseth you, despiseth Me. And he that despiseth Me, despiseth Him that sent Me (*S. Luke* x. 16).

And if he will not hear them : tell the church. And if he will not hear the church, let him be to thee as the heathen and publican (*S. Matt.* xviii. 17).

That thou mayst know how thou oughtest to behave thyself in the house of God, which is the church of the living God, the pillar and ground of the truth (1 *Tim.* iii. 15).

Mutual and Intercessory Prayer.

Q. What is meant by the Communion of Saints?

A. That all the faithful are members of one body, and assist each other by their prayers and good works.

Peter therefore was kept in prison. But prayer was made without ceasing by the church unto God for him (*Acts* xii. 5).

We give thanks to God always for you all ; making a remembrance of you in our prayers without ceasing (1 *Thess.* i. 2).

Pray one for another, that you may be saved. For the continual prayer of a just man availeth much (*S. James* v. 16).

When Moses lifted up his hands, Israel overcame ; but if he let them down a little, Amalec overcame (*Exod.* xvii. 11).

And again the Lord said to Moses : I see that this people is stiff-necked. Let Me alone, that My wrath may be kindled against them, and that I may destroy them, and I will make of thee a great nation. But Moses besought the Lord his God, saying: Why, O Lord, is Thy indignation enkindled against Thy people, whom Thou hast brought out of the land of Egypt, with great power, and with a mighty hand? Let not the Egyptians say, I beseech Thee : He craftily brought them out, that He might kill them in the mountains, and destroy them from the earth ; let Thy anger cease, and be appeased upon the wickedness of Thy people. Remember Abraham, Isaac, and Israel, Thy servants, to whom Thou sworest by Thy ownself, saying : I will multiply your seed as the stars of heaven : and this whole land that I have spoken of, I will give to your seed, and you shall possess it for ever. And the Lord was appeased from doing the evil which He had spoken against His people (*Exod.* xxxii. 9).

They forgot God, who saved them, who had done great things in Egypt, wondrous works in the land of Cham: terrible things in the Red Sea. And He said that He would destroy them: had not Moses His chosen stood before Him in the breach : to turn away His wrath, lest He should destroy them (*Ps.* cv. 21).

And the Lord said to Moses : Get ye out from the midst of this multitude, this moment will I destroy them. And as they were lying on the ground, Moses said to Aaron : Take the censer, and putting fire in it from the altar, put incense upon it, and go quickly to the people to pray for them: for already wrath is gone out from the Lord, and the plague rageth. When Aaron had done this, and had run to the midst of the multitude which the burning fire was now destroying, he offered the incense : and standing between the dead and the living, he prayed for the people, and the plague ceased (*Num.* xvi. 44).

Q. And have we any communion with the saints in Heaven?

A. Yes; we communicate with them as our fellow members, under the same head Jesus Christ; and are helped by their prayers.

So I say to you, there shall be joy before the Angels of God upon one sinner doing penance (*S. Luke* xv. 10).

And when he had opened the fifth seal, I saw under the altar the souls of them that were slain for the word of God, and for the testimony which they held. And they cried with a loud voice, saying: How long, O Lord (holy and true), dost thou not judge and revenge our blood on them that dwell on the earth?

And white robes were given to every one of them one : and it was said to them, that they should rest yet for a little time, till their fellow-servants, and their brethren, who are to be slain, even as they, should be filled up (*Apoc.* vi. 9).

And another Angel came, and stood before the altar, having a golden censer : and there was given to him much incense, that he should offer of the prayers of all saints upon the golden altar, which is before the throne of God. And the smoke of the incense of the prayers of the saints ascended up before God, from the hand of the Angel (*Apoc.* viii. 3).

When thou didst pray with tears, and didst bury the dead, and didst leave thy dinner, and hide the dead by day in thy house, and bury them by night, I offered thy prayer to the Lord (*Tobias* xii. 12).

Then Onias answering, said : This is a lover of his brethren, and of the people of Israel : this is he that prayeth much for the people, and for all the holy city, Jeremias the prophet of God (2 *Macc.* xv. 14).

Q. And are the souls in Purgatory helped by our prayers?

A. Yes; for "it is a holy and wholesome thought to pray for the dead, that they may be loosed from sins" (2 *Macc.* xii. 46).

Q. What do you mean by Purgatory?

A. A place where souls suffer for a time on account of their sins.

Q. What souls go to Purgatory?

A. Those souls which depart this life in venial sin; or which have not fully paid the debt of temporal punishment due to their sins, the guilt of which has been forgiven.

Q. What do you mean by temporal punishment?

A. That which will have an end, either in this world or in the world to come.

Q. Have you any proof from Scripture that there is a Purgatory?

A. Yes; the Scripture teaches that God will render to every man according to his

Be at agreement with thy adversary betimes, whilst thou art in the way with him: lest perhaps the adversary deliver thee to the judge, and the judge deliver thee to the officer, and thou be cast into prison. Amen I say to thee, thou shalt not go out from thence till thou repay the last farthing (*S. Matt.* v. 25).

Now if any man build upon this foundation, gold, silver, precious stones, wood, hay, stubble: Every man's work shall be manifest: for the day of the Lord shall declare it, because it shall be revealed in fire: and the fire shall try every man's work, of what sort it is. If any man's work abide, which he hath built thereupon: he shall receive a reward. If any man's work burn, he shall suffer loss: but he himself shall be saved, yet so as by fire (1 *Cor.* iii. 12).

works, and that nothing defiled can enter Heaven ; and that some Christians shall be saved, yet so as by fire (1 *Cor.* iii. 15).

THE TENTH ARTICLE.

Q. What is the tenth article of the Creed?
A. The forgiveness of sins.

Q. What is meant by this article ?
A. That there is in the Church of God forgiveness of sins, for such as properly apply for it.

Q. To whom has Christ given power to forgive sins ?
A. To the Apostles and their successors, the Bishops and Priests of His Church.

For all have sinned ; and do need the glory of God (*Rom.* iii. 23).
If we say that we have no sin ; we deceive ourselves, and the truth is not in us. If we confess our sins ; He is faithful and just, to forgive us our sins and to cleanse us from all iniquity (1 *S. John* i. 8).
For in many things we all offend (*S. James* iii. 2).
For this is My blood of the New Testament : which shall be shed for many unto remission of sins (*S. Matt.* xxvi. 28).
In whom we have redemption through His blood, the remission of sins (*Col.* i. 14).
Be it known therefore to you, men brethren, that through Him forgiveness of sins is preached to you : and from all the things, from which you could not be justified by the law of Moses (*Acts* xiii. 38).
My little children, these things I write to you that you may not sin. But if any man sin, we have an advocate with the Father, Jesus Christ the just. And He is the propitiation for our sins : and not for ours only, but also for those of the whole world (1 *S. John* ii. 1).

He said therefore to them again : Peace be to you. As the Father has sent Me, I also send you. When He had said this, He breathed on them ; and He said to them : Receive ye the Holy Ghost : whose sins ye shall forgive, they are forgiven them ; and whose sins you shall retain, they are retained (*S. John* xx. 21).

Whether is easier, to say, Thy sins are forgiven thee : or to say, Arise and walk ? But that you may know that the Son of Man hath power on earth to forgive sins, (then saith He to the man sick of the palsy), Arise, take up thy bed, and go into thy house (*S. Matt.* ix. 5).

Original Sin.

Wherefore as by one man sin entered into this world, and by sin death : and so death passed upon all men in whom all have sinned (*Rom.* v. 12).

Therefore as by the offence of one, unto all men to condemnation : so also by the justice of one, unto all men to justification of life. For as by the disobedience of one man, many were made sinners : so also by the obedience of one, many shall be made just (*Rom.* v. 18).

For by a man came death, and by a man the resurrection of the dead. And as in Adam all die, so also in Christ all shall be made alive (1 *Cor.* xv. 21).

Actual Sin.

The soul that sinneth, the same shall die : the son shall not bear the iniquity of the father, and the father shall not bear the iniquity of the son : the justice of the just shall be upon him, and the wickedness of the wicked shall be upon him But if the wicked do penance for all his sins, which he hath committed, and keep all My commandments, and do judgment, and justice, living he shall live, and shall not die (*Ezechiel* xviii. 20).

Q. By what sacraments are sins fogiven ?
A. Principally by Baptism and Penance.

Q. What is sin ?
A. An offence against God, or any thought, word, or deed, against the law of God.

Q. How many kinds of sin are there?
A. Two; original and actual.

Q. What is original sin ?
A. It is the sin in which we were conceived.

Thy own wickedness shall reprove thee, and thy apostasy shall rebuke thee. Know thou, and see that it is an evil and a bitter thing for thee, to have left the Lord thy God, and that My fear is not with thee, saith the Lord the God of hosts. Of old time thou hast broken My yoke, thou hast burst My bands, and thou saidst : I will not serve (*Jer.* ii. 19).

Sins of Thought.

But I say to you, that whosoever shall look on a woman to lust after her, hath already committed adultery with her in his heart (*S. Matt.* v. 28).

For from the heart come forth evil thoughts, murders, adulteries, fornications, thefts, false testimonies, blasphemies. These are the things that defile a man (*S. Matt.* xv. 19).

Sins of Word.

If any man offend not in word : the same is a perfect man (*S. James* iii. 2).

But I say unto you, that every idle word that men shall speak, they shall render an account for it in the day of judgment. For by thy words thou shalt be justified, and by thy words thou shalt be condemned (*S. Matt.* xii. 36).

Q. How came we to be conceived in sin ?
A. Through Adam's sin, when he ate the forbidden fruit.

And to Adam He said : Because thou hast hearkened to the voice of thy wife, and hast eaten of the tree whereof I commanded thee that thou shouldst not eat, cursed is the earth in thy work ; with labour and toil shalt thou eat thereof all the days of thy life. Thorns and thistles shall it bring forth to thee; and thou shalt eat the herbs of the earth. In the sweat of thy face shalt thou eat bread till thou return to the earth, out of which thou wast taken : for dust thou art, and unto dust thou shalt return (*Gen.* iii. 17).

Q. Are all mankind conceived in sin ?

A. Yes ; all mankind, except the Blessed Virgin, who by a special privilege and grace of God, through the merits of her Son, was conceived without the stain of original sin.

And the Angel being come in, said unto her : Hail, full of grace, the Lord is with thee : Blessed art thou among women (*S. Luke* i. 28).

And a great sign appeared in Heaven : A woman clothed with the sun, and the moon under her feet, and on her head a crown of twelve stars (*Apoc.* xii. 1).

Thou art all fair, O my love, and there is not a spot in thee (*Canticles* iv. 7).

Q. What is actual sin ?

A. Every sin which we ourselves commit.

Be not deceived, God is not mocked. For what things a man shall sow, those also shall he reap. For he that soweth in his flesh, of the flesh also shall reap corruption. But he that soweth in the spirit, of the spirit shall reap life everlasting (*Gal.* vi. 7).

Q. How is actual sin divided ?

A. Into mortal sin and venial sin.

Q. What is mortal sin ?

A. It is a grievous offence against God.

Q. Why is it called mortal ?

A. Because it kills the soul and deserves hell.

Q. How does mortal sin kill the soul ?

A. By depriving the soul of its supernatural life, which is the grace of God.

For there is no respect of persons with God. For whosoever have sinned without the law, shall perish without the law : and whosever have sinned in the law, shall be judged by the law (*Rom.* ii. 11).

For the wages of sin, is death. But the grace of God, life everlasting in Jesus Christ our Lord (*Rom.* vi. 23).

And they violated Me among My people, for a handful of barley, and a piece of bread (*Ezechiel* xiii. 19).

Behold all souls are Mine : as the soul of the father, so also the soul of the son is Mine : the soul that sinneth, the same shall die (*Ezechiel* xviii. 4).

Q. What is venial sin?
A. That sin which does not kill the soul, yet displeases God.

Q. Why is it called venial?
A. Because it is more easily pardoned than mortal sin.

For a just man shall fall seven times, and shall rise again : but the wicked shall fall down into evil (*Prov.* xxiv. 16).

Shall man be justified in comparison of God, or shall a man be more pure than his Maker? Behold they that serve Him are not steadfast, and in His angels He found wickedness : how much more shall they that dwell in houses of clay, who have an earthly foundation, be consumed as with the moth? (*Job* iv. 17.)

What is man that he should be without spot, and he that is born of a woman that he should appear just? Behold among His saints none is unchangeable, and the heavens are not pure in His sight (*Job* xv. 14).

If we say that we have no sin ; we deceive ourselves, and the truth is not in us (1 *S. John* i. 8).

And enter not into judgment with Thy servant : for in Thy sight no man living shall be justified (*Ps.* cxlii. 2).

And why seest thou the mote that is in thy brother's eye, and seest not the beam that is in thy own eye? (*S. Matt.* vii. 3.)

THE ELEVENTH ARTICLE.

Q. What is the eleventh article of the Creed?
A. The resurrection of the body.

Q. What means the resurrection of the body?
A. That we shall all rise again with the same bodies at the day of judgment.

Amen, amen, I say unto you, that the hour cometh, and now is, when the dead shall hear the voice of the Son of God, and they that hear shall live (*S. John* v. 25).

Jesus said to her : I am the resurrection and the life : he that believeth in Me although he be dead, shall live (*S. John* xi. 25).

For if the dead rise not again, neither is Christ risen again. And if Christ be not risen again, your faith is vain, for you are yet in your sins. Then they also that are fallen

E

asleep in Christ, are perished. If in this life only we have hope in Christ, we are of all men most miserable (1 *Cor.* xv. 16).

Behold I tell you a mystery. We shall indeed rise again : but we shall not all be changed. In a moment, in the twinkling of an eye, at the last trumpet : for the trumpet shall sound, and the dead shall rise again incorruptible : and we shall be changed. For this corruptible must put on incorruption ; and this mortal must put on immortality (1 *Cor.* xv. 51).

For I know that my Redeemer liveth, and in the last day I shall rise out of the earth. And I shall be clothed again with my skin, and in my flesh I shall see my God (*Job* xix. 25).

THE TWELFTH ARTICLE.

Q. What is the twelfth article of the Creed?
A. Life everlasting.

Q. What means this article?
A. That the good shall live for ever happy in Heaven.

Q. What is the happiness of Heaven?
A. To see, love, and enjoy God for evermore.

Wonder not at this, for the hour cometh wherein all that are in the graves shall hear the voice of the Son of God. And they that have done good things, shall come forth unto the resurrection of life ; but they that have done evil, unto the resurrection of judgment (*S. John* v. 28).

And many of those that sleep in the dust of the earth, shall awake : some unto life everlasting, and others unto reproach, to see it always (*Dan.* xii. 2).

Blessed are they that wash their robes in the blood of the Lamb : that they may have a right to the tree of life, and may enter in by the gates into the city (*Apoc.* xxii. 14)

' Q. And shall not the wicked also live for ever?
A. They shall live and be punished for ever in the flames of hell.

And the sea gave up the dead that were in it, and death and hell gave up their dead that were in them : and they were judged every one according to their works. And hell and death were cast into the pool of fire. This is the second death (*Apoc.* xx. 13.)

CHAPTER III.

HOPE.—THE LORD'S PRAYER.

Q. Will faith alone save us?
A. No; it will not without good works.

What Faith is.

Now faith is the substance of things to be hoped for, the evidence of things that appear not. For by this the ancients obtained a testimony. By faith we understand that the world was framed by the word of God; that from invisible things visible things might be made (*Heb.* xi. 1).

Necessity of Faith.

But without faith it is impossible to please God. For he that cometh to God, must believe that He is, and is a rewarder to them that seek Him (*Heb.* xi. 6).

But that in the law no man is justified with God, it is manifest: because the just man liveth by faith (*Gal.* iii. 11).

By whom also we have access through faith into this grace, wherein we stand, and glory in the hope of the glory of the sons of God (*Rom.* v. 2).

For whatsoever is born of God, overcometh the world: and this is the victory which overcometh the world, our faith (1 *S. John* v. 4).

Faith a virtue to be guarded by Prayer.

Having faith and a good conscience, which some rejecting have made shipwreck concerning the faith (1 *Tim.* i. 19).

And Jesus answering said to them: Amen I say to you, if you shall have faith, and stagger not, not only this of the fig-tree shall you do, but also

E 2

if you shall say to this mountain,
Take up and cast thyself into the
sea, it shall be done (*Matt.* xxi. 21).

Dearly beloved, taking all care to
write unto you concerning your common salvation, I was under a necessity to write unto you : to beseech
you to contend earnestly for the
faith once delivered to the saints
(*S. Jude* 3).

And the apostles said to the Lord :
Increase our faith (*S. Luke* xvii. 5).

And immediately the father of the
boy crying out, with tears said : I
do believe, Lord : help my unbelief
(*S. Mark* ix. 23).

Not sufficient of itself.

So faith also, if it have not works,
is dead in itself. But some man will
say : Thou hast faith, and I have
works ; shew me thy faith without
works : and I will shew thee, by
works, my faith. Thou believest
that there is one God. Thou dost
well : the devils also believe and
tremble. But wilt thou know, O
vain man, that faith without works is
dead ? (*S. James* ii. 17.)

And if I should have prophecy,
and should know all mysteries, and
all knowledge, and if I should have
all faith, so that I could remove
mountains, and have not charity, I
am nothing (1 *Cor.* xiii. 2).

Many will say to me in that day :
Lord, Lord, have we not prophesied
in Thy name, and cast out devils in
Thy name, and done many miracles
in Thy name ? And then will I profess unto them, I never knew you :
depart from Me, you that work
iniquity (*S. Matt.* vii. 22).

For in Christ Jesus neither cir-
cumsion availeth any thing, nor un-
circumcision : but faith that worketh
by charity (*Gal.* v. 6).

Q. Can we of ourselves do any good work towards our salvation?

A. No ; we cannot without the help of God's grace.

Wherefore I give you to understand, that no man, speaking by the spirit of God, saith anathema to Jesus. And no man can say, the Lord Jesus, but by the Holy Ghost (1 *Cor.* xii. 3).

But by the grace of God, I am what I am : and His grace in me hath not been void, but I have laboured more abundantly than all they : yet not I, but the grace of God with me (1 *Cor.* xv. 10).

For it is God who worketh in you, both to will and to accomplish, according to His good will (*Phil.* ii. 13).

No man can come to Me, except the Father, who hath sent Me, draw him, and I will raise him up in the last day (*S. John* vi. 44).

I am the vine ; you the branches : he that abideth in Me, and I in him, the same beareth much fruit : for without Me you can do nothing (*S. John* xv. 5).

And we helping do exhort you, that you receive not the grace of God in vain (2 *Cor.* vi. 1).

Unless the Lord build the house, they labour in vain that build it. Unless the Lord keep the city, he watcheth in vain that keepeth it (*Ps.* cxxvi. 1).

I have planted, Apollo watered, but God gave the increase. Therefore neither he that planteth is any thing, nor he that watereth ; but God that giveth the increase (1 *Cor.* iii. 6).

Being justified freely by His grace, through the redemption that is in Christ Jesus (*Rom.* iii. 24).

Wherefore, brethren, labour the more that by good works you may make sure your calling and election. For doing these things, you shall not sin at any time (2 *S. Pet.* i. 10).

Q. What is grace?
A. Grace is a super-
natural gift of God,
freely bestowed upon
us, for our sanctification
and salvation.

Habitual or Sanctifying Grace.

And hope confoundeth not; because the charity of God is poured
forth in our hearts, by the Holy
Ghost who is given to us (*Rom.* v.
5).

Let your loins be girt, and lamps
burning in your hands (*S. Luke* xii.
35).

And he saith to him : Friend, how
camest thou in hither not having
a wedding garment? But he was
silent. Then the king said to the
waiters : Bind his hands and feet,
and cast him into the exterior darkness : there shall be weeping and
gnashing of teeth (*Matt.* xxii. 12).

Actual or Helping Grace.

Let no temptation take hold on
you, but such as is human. And
God is faithful, who will not suffer
you to be tempted above that which
you are able : but will make also
with temptation issue, that you may
be able to bear it (1 *Cor.* x. 13).

And He said to me : My grace is
sufficient for thee : for power is made
perfect in infirmity (2 *Cor.* xii. 9).

I can do all things in Him who
strengtheneth me (*Phil.* iv. 13).

Q. How may we ob-
tain God's grace?
A. By prayer and the
holy sacraments.

For the continual prayer of a just
man availeth much (*S. James* v. 16).

And I say to you, Ask, and it
shall be given you : seek, and you
shall find : knock, and it shall be
opened to you (*S. Luke* xi. 9).

*The Sacraments means of Grace and
Refreshment for those within the
Fold.*

I am the door. By Me, if any
man enter in, he shall be saved :
and he shall go in, and go out, and
shall find pastures (*S. John* x. 9).

Q. What is prayer?
A. It is the raising up of our minds and hearts to God.

Q. How do we raise up our minds and hearts to God?
A. By thinking of God, by adoring and praising Him, and by begging of Him all blessings for soul and body.

Q. Do those pray well, who at their prayers think not of God or of what they say?
A. No; if their distractions are wilful, they do not pray well, but they offend God.

Q. Which is the best of all prayers?
A. The Lord's prayer.

Q. Who made this prayer?
A. Christ our Lord.

Say the Lord's prayer.
Our Father who art in Heaven, hallowed be Thy name; Thy kingdom come; Thy will be done on earth as it is in

But thou when thou shalt pray, enter into thy chamber, and having shut the door, pray to thy Father in secret: and thy Father who seeth in secret will repay thee (*S. Matt.* vi. 6).

Prayer is good with fasting and alms, more than to lay up treasures of gold (*Tobias* xii. 8).

Let nothing hinder thee from praying always, and be not afraid to be justified even to death: for the reward of God continueth for ever. Before prayer prepare thy soul: and be not as a man that tempteth God (*Ecclus.* xviii. 22).

You ask, and receive not: because you ask amiss (*S. James* iv. 3).

My heart grew hot within me: and in my meditation a fire shall flame out (*Ps.* xxxviii. 4).

With desolation is all the land made desolate: because there is none that considereth in the heart (*Jer.* xii. 11).

And when you are praying, speak not much, as the heathens. For they think that in their much speaking they may be heard. Be not you therefore like to them, for your Father knoweth what is needful for you before you ask Him. Thus therefore shall you pray: Our Father who art in Heaven, hallowed be thy name. Thy kingdom come. Thy will be done on earth as it is in Heaven. Give us this day our supersubstantial bread. And forgive us our debts, as we also forgive our

Heaven. Give us this day our daily bread ; and forgive us our trespasses, as we forgive them that trespass against us : and lead us not into temptation ; but deliver us from evil. Amen.

Q. Who is it that is here called our Father?
A. God.

Q. Why is He called our Father ?
A. Because He made us all, and loves and preserves us all.

Q. Is He especially the Father of Christians ?
A. Yes ; because by baptism He has made us His children in Jesus Christ.

Q. Why do we say our Father, and not My Father?
A. Because we are not to pray for ourselves only, but for all others.

debtors. And lead us not into temptation. But deliver us from evil. Amen (*S. Matt.* vi. 7).

And it came to pass, that as He was in a certain place praying, when He ceased, one of His disciples said to Him : Lord, teach us to pray, as John also taught his disciples. And he said to them : When you pray, say : Father, hallowed be Thy name. Thy kingdom come (*S. Luke* xi. 1).

As a father hath compassion on his children, so hath the Lord compassion on them that fear Him : for He knoweth our frame. He remembereth that we are dust (*Ps.* cii. 13).

The son honoureth the father, and the servant his master : if then I be a father, where is My honour? and if I be a master, where is My fear? saith the Lord of hosts (*Mal.* i. 6).

And call no man your father upon the earth : for one is your Father, who is in Heaven (*S. Matt.* xxiii. 9).

For you have not received the spirit of bondage again in fear : but you have received the spirit of adoption of sons, whereby we cry : Abba (Father). For the Spirit Himself giveth testimony to our spirit, that we are the sons of God. And if sons, heirs also : heirs indeed of God, and joint heirs with Christ (*Rom.* viii. 15).

But be not you called Rabbi. For one is your master, and all you are brethren. And call none your father upon earth : for one is your Father who is in Heaven (*S. Matt.* xxiii. 8).

For I wished myself to be an anathema from Christ, for my brethren, who are my kinsmen according to the flesh (*Rom.* ix. 3).

In this we have known the charity of God, because He hath laid down His life for us : and we ought to lay down our lives for the brethren (1 *S. John* iii. 16).

Q. What do we pray for, when we say, Hallowed be Thy name?
A. We pray that God may be praised, loved, and served by all His creatures.

O Lord our God, how admirable is Thy name in the whole earth ! For Thy magnificence is elevated above the heavens (*Ps.* viii. 2).

Praise the Lord, ye children : praise ye the name of the Lord. Blessed be the name of the Lord, from henceforth now and for ever. From the rising of the sun unto the going down of the same, the name of the Lord is worthy of praise (*Ps.* cxii. 1).

Not to us, O Lord, not to us ; but to Thy name give glory (*Ps.* cxiii. 1).

Kingdom of God—Heaven.

Q. What do we pray for, when we say, Thy kingdom come?
A. We pray that God may come and reign in our hearts by His grace, and may bring us all hereafter to His heavenly kingdom.

And he said to Jesus : Lord, remember me when thou shalt come into Thy kingdom. And Jesus said to him : Amen I say to thee, this day thou shalt be with Me in Paradise (*S. Luke* xxiii. 42).

Then shall the just shine as the sun, in the kingdom of their Father (*S. Matt.* xiii. 43).

And immediately I was in the spirit : and behold there was a throne set in Heaven, and upon the throne One sitting. And He that sat, was to the sight like the jasper and the sardine-stone : and there was a rainbow round about the throne, in sight like unto an emerald. And round about the throne were four-and-twenty seats : and upon the seats, four-and-twenty ancients sitting, clothed in white garments, and on their heads were crowns of gold. And from the throne proceeded lightnings and voices and thunders : and there were seven lamps burning before the throne, which are the seven spirits of God. And in the sight of the throne was as it were a sea of glass like to crystal : and in the midst of the throne and round about the throne were four living creatures full of eyes before and behind (*Apoc.* iv. 2).

And above the firmament that was over their heads, was the likeness of a throne, as the appearance of the sapphire-stone, and upon the likeness of the throne, was a likeness as of the appearance of a man above upon it. And I saw as it were the resemblance of amber, as the appearance of fire within it round about : from His loins and upward, and from His loins downward, I saw as it were the resemblance of fire shining round about. As the appearance of the rainbow when it is in a cloud on a rainy day: this was the appearance of the brightness round about (*Ezek.* i. 26).

And I dispose to you, as My Father hath disposed to Me, a kingdom : that you may eat and drink at My table in My kingdom : and may sit upon thrones judging the twelve tribes of Israel (*S. Luke* xxii. 29).

Kingdom of God the Church.

Again the kingdom of heaven is like to a net cast into the sea, and gathering together of all kind of fishes. Which, when it was filled, they drew out, and sitting by the shore, they chose out the good into vessels, but the bad they cast forth. So shall it be at the end of the world. The Angels shall go out, and shall separate the wicked from among the just (*S. Matt.* xiii. 47).

Another parable He proposed

unto them, saying: The kingdom of heaven is like to a grain of mustard seed, which a man took and sowed in his field : which is the least indeed of all seeds: but when it is grown up, it is greater than all herbs, and becometh a tree, so that the birds of the air come, and dwell in the branches thereof (*S. Matt.* xiii. 31).

Kingdom of God's Grace within us.

Another parable he spoke to them: The kingdom of heaven is like to leaven, which a woman took and hid in three measures of meal, until the whole was leavened (*S. Matt.* xiii. 33).

Neither shall they say: Behold here, or behold there. For lo, the kingdom of God is within you (*S. Luke* xvii. 21).

Q. What do we pray for, when we say, Thy will be done on earth, as it is in Heaven?

A. We pray that God may enable us, by His grace, to do His will in all things, as the blessed do in Heaven.

Then said I : Behold I come : in the head of the book it is written of Me : that I should do Thy will, O God (*Heb.* x. 7).

Jesus saith to them : My meat is to do the will of Him that sent Me, that I may perfect His work (*S. John* iv. 34).

And going a little further, He fell upon His face, praying, and saying : My Father, if it be possible, let this chalice pass from Me. Nevertheless, not as I will, but as Thou wilt (*S. Matt.* xxvi. 39).

So Samuel told him all the words and did not hide them from him. And he answered : It is the Lord : let Him do what is good in His sight (1 *Kings* iii. 18).

For it is better for us to die in battle, than to see the evils of our nation, and of the holies : nevertheless as it shall be the will of God in heaven, so be it done (1 *Macc.* iii. 60).

Q. What do we pray for, when we say, Give us this day our daily bread?

A. We pray that God may give us daily all that is necessary for our souls and bodies.

And the tempter coming, said to Him : If Thou be the Son of God, command that these stones be made bread. Who answered and said : It is written, Not in bread alone doth man live, but in every word that proceedeth from the mouth of God (*S. Matt.* iv. 3).

Consider the ravens, for they sow not, neither do they reap, neither have they store-house nor barn, and God feedeth them. How much are you more valuable than they? (*S. Luke* xii. 24.)

Who giveth to beasts their food : and to the young ravens that call upon Him (*Ps.* cxlvi. 9).

All expect of Thee that Thou give them food in season. When Thou givest to them they shall gather up : when Thou openest Thy hand, they shall all be filled with good (*Ps.* ciii. 27).

Q. What do we pray for, when we say, Forgive us our trespasses, as we forgive them that trespass against us?

A. We pray that God may forgive us our sins, as we forgive others the injuries they do us.

Then his lord called him ; and said to him : Thou wicked servant, I forgave thee all the debt, because thou besoughtest me : shouldst not thou then have had compassion also on thy fellow-servant, even as I had compassion on thee? And his Lord being angry, delivered him to the torturers until he should pay all the debt. So also shall My heavenly Father do to you, if you forgive not every one his brother from your hearts (*S. Matt.* xviii. 32).

If therefore thou offer thy gift at the altar, and there thou remember that thy brother hath any thing against thee ; leave there thy offering before the altar, and go first to be reconciled to thy brother : and then coming thou shalt offer thy gift (*S. Matt.* v. 23).

Q. What do we pray

A hard heart shall fare evil at the

for, when we say, Lead us not into temptation?

A. We pray that God may give us grace not to yield to temptation.

last : and he that loveth danger shall perish in it (*Ecclus.* iii. 27).

Jesus said to him: It is written, again : Thou shalt not tempt the Lord thy God (*S. Matt.* iv. 7).

Blessed is the man that endureth temptation ; for when he hath been proved, he shall receive the crown of life, which God hath promised to them that love Him. Let no man, when he is tempted, say that he is tempted by God. For God is not a tempter of evils, and He tempteth no man. But every man is tempted by his own concupiscence, being drawn away and allured (*S. James* i. 12).

Q. What do we pray for, when we say, Deliver us from evil?

A. We pray that God may free us from all evil of soul and body.

If I take my wings early in the morning, and dwell in the uttermost parts of the sea: even there also shall Thy hand lead me: and Thy right hand shall hold me (*Ps.* cxxxviii. 9).

He will overshadow thee with His shoulders : and under His wings thou shalt trust. His truth shall compass thee with a shield: thou shalt not be afraid of the terror of the night. Of the arrow that flieth in the day, of the business that walketh about in the dark : of invasion, or of the noonday devil. A thousand shall fall at thy side, and ten thousand at thy right hand : but it shall not come nigh thee (*Ps.* xc. 4).

Come to Me, all you that labour, and are burdened, and I will refresh you (*S. Matt.* xi. 28).

For though I should walk in the midst of the shadow of death, I will fear no evils, for Thou art with me (*Ps.* xxii. 4).

Q. May we ask the Saints and Angels to pray for us?

A. Yes, we may.

Are they not all ministering spirits, sent to minister for them, who shall receive the inheritance of salvation ? (*Heb.* i. 14.)

Q. Why do we ask the Saints and Angels to pray for us?

A. Because they are our brethren, and their prayers have great power with God.

Q. How do you prove that the Saints and Angels know what passes on earth?

A. By the words of Christ: "There shall be joy before the Angels of God upon one sinner doing penance" (*S. Luke* xv. 10).

Q. What is the prayer to our Blessed Lady which the Church teaches?

A. The Hail Mary.

Say the Hail Mary.

Hail Mary, full of grace, the Lord is with thee: blessed art thou amongst women, and blessed is the fruit of thy womb, Jesus. Holy Mary, Mother of God, pray for us sinners, now, and at the hour of our death. Amen.

Q. Who made the first part of the Hail Mary?

Who have received the law by the disposition of Angels, and have not kept it (*Acts* vii. 53).

For He hath given His angels charge over thee; to keep thee in all thy ways. In their hands they shall bear thee up: lest thou dash thy foot against a stone (*Ps.* xc. 11).

The angel that delivereth me from all evils, bless these boys: and let my name be called upon them, and the names of my fathers Abraham and Isaac, and may they grow into a multitude upon the earth (*Gen.* xlviii. 16).

See that you despise not one of these little ones: for I say to you, that their angels in Heaven always see the face of My Father who is in Heaven (*S. Matt.* xviii. 10).

And in the sixth month, the angel Gabriel was sent from God into a city of Galilee, called Nazareth, to a virgin espoused to a man whose name was Joseph, of the house of David: and the virgin's name was Mary. And the Angel being come in, said unto her: Hail, full of grace, the Lord is with thee: Blessed art thou among women (*S. Luke* i. 26).

And it came to pass; that when Elizabeth heard the salutation of Mary, the infant leaped in her womb. And Elizabeth was filled with the Holy Ghost: and she cried out with a loud voice, and said: Blessed art thou among women, and blessed is the fruit of thy womb. And whence is this to me,

A. The angel Gabriel and St. Elizabeth, inspired by the Holy Ghost.

Q. Who made the last part?

A. The Church of God, guided by the same Holy Spirit.

Q. Why do we say the Hail Mary so often?

A. To put us in mind of the Incarnation of God the Son, and to honour His blessed Mother.

Q. Why does the Catholic Church show such devotion to the Blessed Virgin?

A. Because she is the Immaculate Mother of God.

that the mother of my Lord should come to me? For behold as soon as the voice of thy salutation sounded in my ears, the infant in my womb leaped for joy. And blessed art thou that hast believed, because those things shall be accomplished that were spoken to thee by the Lord (*S. Luke* i. 41).

Because He hath regarded the humility of His handmaid : for behold from henceforth all generations shall call me blessed (*S. Luke* i. 48).

———◆———

CHAPTER IV.

CHARITY.—THE TEN COMMANDMENTS.

Q. How many commandments are there?

A. Ten.

Say the Ten com-
mandments.

I am the Lord thy
God, who brought thee
out of the land of
Egypt, and out of the
house of bondage.

1. Thou shalt not
have strange Gods be-
fore Me.   Thou shalt
not make to thyself any
graven thing, nor the
likeness of any thing that
is in Heaven above or
in the earth beneath,
nor of those things that
are in the waters under
the earth ; thou shalt
not adore them   nor
serve them.

2. Thou shalt not
take the name of the
Lord thy God in vain.

3. Remember   that
thou keep holy the Sab-
bath day.   .

4. Honour thy father
and thy mother.

5. Thou shalt not kill.

6. Thou   shalt   not
commit adultery.

7. Thou   shalt   not
steal.

8. Thou   shalt   not
bear false witness against
thy neighbour.

9. Thou shalt not covet
thy neighbour's wife.

10. Thou   shalt   not
covet thy neighbour's
goods.

Q. Who gave the ten
commandments ?

A. God gave them on
Mount Sinai.

And the Lord came down upon
Mount Sinai, in the very top of the
mount, and He called Moses unto
the top thereof.   And when he was
gone up thither, He said unto him :

Go down, and charge the people : lest they should have a mind to pass the limits to see the Lord, and a very great multitude of them should perish (*Exod.* xix. 20).

Q. Are we bound to keep them ?

A. We are ; for our Lord says, "If thou wilt enter into life, keep the commandments" (*S. Matt.* xix. 17).

Do not think that I am come to destroy the law, or the prophets. I am not come to destroy, but to fulfil. For amen I say unto you, till heaven and earth pass, one jot, or one tittle shall not pass from the law, till all be fulfilled (*S. Matt.* v. 17).

Keep the precepts of the Lord thy God, and the testimonies and ceremonies which He hath commanded thee (*Deut.* vi. 17).

And He will be merciful to us, if we keep and do all His precepts before the Lord our God, as He hath commanded us (*Deut.* vi. 25).

Lay up these My words in your hearts and minds, and hang them for a sign on your hands, and place them between your eyes. Teach your children that they meditate on them, when thou sittest in thy house, and when thou walkest on the way, and when thou liest down and risest up. Thou shalt write them upon the posts and the doors of thy house (*Deut.* xi. 18).

If you love Me, keep My commandments (*S. John* xiv. 15).

And by this we know that we have known Him, if we keep His commandments. He who saith that he knoweth Him, and keepeth not His commandments, is a liar, and the truth is not in him : but he that keepeth His word, in him in very deed the charity of God is perfected : and by this we know that we are in Him (1 *S. John* ii. 3).

Now whosoever shall keep the whole law, but offend in one point, is become guilty of all (*S. James* ii. 10).

F

Q. What do these commandments teach us?

A. They teach us to avoid evil and do good.

Decline from evil and do good, and dwell for ever and ever (*Ps.* xxxvi. 27).

For My people have done two evils. They have forsaken Me, the fountain of living water, and have digged to themselves cisterns, broken cisterns, that can hold no water (*Jer.* ii. 13).

Hating that which is evil, cleaving to that which is good (*Rom.* xii. 9).

Turn away from evil and do good : seek after peace and pursue it. The eyes of the Lord are upon the just : and His ears unto their prayers. But the countenance of the Lord is against them that do evil things : to cut off the remembrance of them from the earth (*Ps.* xxxiii. 15).

Q. What is the first commandment?

A. Thou shalt not have strange Gods before Me. Thou shalt not make to thyself any graven thing, nor the likeness of any thing that is in Heaven above, or in the earth beneath, nor of those things that are in the waters under the earth ; thou shalt not adore them nor serve them.

And one of them, a doctor of the law, asked Him, tempting Him : Master, which is the great commandment in the law? Jesus said to him : Thou shalt love the Lord thy God with thy whole heart, and with thy whole soul, and with thy whole mind. This is the greatest and the first commandment. And the second is like to this : Thou shalt love thy neighbour as thyself. On these two commandments dependeth the whole law and the prophets (*S. Matt.* xxii. 35).

Q. What are we commanded to do by the first commandment?

A. We are commanded to believe in the one true and living God ; to hope in Him, to love Him, and to serve Him all our days.

And now, Israel, what doth the Lord thy God require of thee, but that thou fear the Lord thy God, and walk in His ways, and love Him, and serve the Lord thy God, with all thy heart, and with all thy soul? (*Deut.* x. 12.)

Q. What does the first commandment forbid?

A. The first commandment forbids us to worship false gods or idols, or to give to any creature whatsoever the honour which is due to God.

The idols of the Gentiles are silver and gold, the works of the hands of men. They have mouths and speak not : they have eyes and see not. They have ears and hear not : they have noses and smell not. They have hands and feel not : they have feet and walk not : neither shall they cry out through their throat. Let them that make them become like unto them : and all such as trust in them (*Ps.* cxiii. 4).

For they have esteemed all the idols of the heathens for gods, which neither have the use of eyes to see, nor noses to draw breath, nor ears to hear, nor fingers of hands to handle, and as for their feet, they are slow to walk. For man made them : and he that borroweth his own breath, fashioned them. For no man can make a god like to himself. For being mortal himself, he formeth a dead thing with his wicked hands. For he is better than they whom he worshippeth, because he indeed hath lived, though he were mortal, but they never. Moreover they worship also the vilest creatures : but things without sense compared to these, are worse than they (*Wisd.* xv. 15).

Being therefore the offspring of God we must not suppose the divinity to be like unto gold or silver, or stone, the graving of art and device of man (*Acts* xvii. 29).

Q. What else is forbidden by the first commandment?

A. All false religions, and all disbelief, or wilful doubt of any article of faith.

But though we, or an angel from Heaven, preach a gospel to you besides that which we have preached to you, let him be anathema. As we said before, so now I say again: If any one preach to you a gospel, besides that which you have received, let him be anathema (*Gal.* i. 8).

That henceforth we be no more children tossed to and fro, and carried about with every wind of doctrine by the wickedness of men, by cunning craftiness by which they lie in wait to deceive (*Eph.* iv. 14).

Hold the form of sound words, which thou hast heard of me in faith, and in the love which is in Christ Jesus. Keep the good thing committed to thy trust by the Holy Ghost, who dwelleth in us (2 *Tim.* i. 13).

And the things, which thou hast heard of me by many witnesses, the same commend to faithful men, who shall be fit to teach others also (2 *Tim.* ii. 2).

A man that is a heretic, after the first and second admonition, avoid: knowing that he, that is such an one, is subverted, and sinneth, being condemned by his own judgment (*Titus* iii. 10).

And Nadab and Abiu, the sons of Aaron, taking their censers, put fire therein, and incense on it, offering before the Lord strange fire : which was not commanded them. And fire coming out from the Lord destroyed them, and they died before the Lord (*Levit.* x. 1).

Sin of Sacrilege.

But the children of Israel transgressed the commandment, and took to their own use of the anathema. For Achan the son of Charmi, the son of Zabdi, the son of Zare of the tribe of Juda, took something of the anathema: and the Lord was angry against the children of Israel (*Josue* vii. 1).

Then Saul said: Bring me the holocaust, and the peace-offerings. And he offered the holocaust. And when he had made an end of offer-

ing the holocaust, behold Samuel
came; and Saul went forth to meet
him and salute him. And Samuel
said to him: What hast thou done?
Saul answered: Because I saw that
the people slipt from me, and thou
wast not come according to the days
appointed, and the Philistines were
gathered together in Machmas, I
said : Now will the Philistines come
down upon me to Galgal, and I
have not appeased the face of the
Lord. Forced by necessity, I offered
the holocaust. And Samuel said to
Saul: Thou hast done foolishly, and
hast not kept the commandments of
the Lord thy God, which He commanded thee. And if thou hadst
not done thus, the Lord would now
have established thy kingdom over
Israel for ever (1 *Kings* xiii. 9).

And he gave a sign the same day,
saying : This shall be the sign, that
the Lord hath spoken : Behold the
altar shall be rent, and the ashes
that are upon it shall be poured out.
And when the king had heard the
word of the man of God, which he
had cried out against the altar in
Bethel, he stretched forth his hand
from the altar, saying : Lay hold on
him. And his hand which he
stretched forth against him withered :
and he was not able to draw it
back again to him (3 *Kings* xiii. 3).

But when he was made strong,
his heart was lifted up to his destruction, and he neglected the Lord his
God : and going into the temple of
the Lord, he had a mind to burn
incense upon the altar of incense.
And immediately Azarias the priest
going in after him, and with him
fourscore priests of the Lord, most
valiant men, withstood the king, and
said : It doth not belong to thee,
Ozias, to burn incense to the Lord,

but to the priests, that is, to the sons of Aaron, who are consecrated for this ministry : go out of the sanctuary, do not despise : for this thing shall not be accounted to thy glory by the Lord God. And Ozias was angry, and holding in his hand the censer to burn incense, threatened the priests. And presently there rose a leprosy in his forehead before the priests, in the house of the Lord at the altar of incense. And Azarias the high-priest, and all the rest of the priests looked upon him, and saw the leprosy in his forehead, and they made haste to thrust him out. Yea himself also being frightened, hasted to go out, because he had quickly felt the stroke of the Lord (2 *Paral.* xxvi. 16).

But Heliodorus executed that which he had resolved on, himself being present in the same place with his guard about the treasury. But the spirit of the almighty God gave a great evidence of His presence, so that all that had presumed to obey him, falling down by the power of God, were struck with fainting and dread. For there appeared to them a horse with a terrible rider upon him, adorned with a very rich covering : and he ran fiercely and struck Heliodorus with his fore-feet, and he that sat upon him, seemed to have armour of gold. Moreover there appeared two other young men beautiful and strong, bright and glorious, and in comely apparel : who stood by him, on either side, and scourged him without ceasing with many stripes. And Heliodorus suddenly fell to the ground, and they took him up covered with great darkness; and having put him into a litter, they carried him out (2 *Mach.* iii. 23).

Q. Does the first commandment forbid any thing else?

A. Yes; dealing with the devil; and inquiring after hidden things, or things to come by fortune-tellers, or superstitious practices.

The soul that shall go aside after magicians and soothsayers, and shall commit fornication with them, I will set my face against that soul, and destroy it out of the midst of its people (*Levit.* xx. 6).

And an angel of the Lord spoke to Elias the Thesbite, saying: Arise, and go up to meet the messengers of the King of Samaria, and say to them : Is there not a God in Israel, that ye go to consult Beelzebub the god of Accaron? Wherefore thus saith the Lord : From the bed, on which thou art gone up, thou shalt not come down, but thou shalt surely die. And Elias went away. And the messengers turned back to Ochozias (4 *Kings* i. 3).

And Saul said to his servants : Seek me a woman that hath a divining spirit, and I will go to her, and inquire by her. And his servants said to him : There is a woman that hath a divining spirit at Endor. Then he disguised himself : and put on other clothes, and he went, and two men with him, and they came to the woman by night, and he said to her : Divine to me by thy divining spirit, and bring me up him whom I shall tell thee. And the woman said to him : Behold thou knowest all that Saul hath done, and how he hath rooted out the magicians and soothsayers from the land : why then dost thou lay a snare for my life, to cause me to be put to death? And Saul swore unto her by the Lord, saying : As the Lord liveth there shall no evil happen to thee for this thing. And the woman said to him : Whom shall I bring up to thee? And he said : Bring me up Samuel. And when the woman saw Samuel, she cried out with a loud voice, and said to Saul : Why hast thou deceived me? for thou art Saul. And the king said to her: Fear not : what hast thou seen? And the woman said to Saul : I saw gods ascending out of the earth. And he said to her : What form is he of? And she said : An old man cometh up, and he is covered with a mantle. And Saul understood that it was Samuel, and he bowed himself with his face to the ground, and adored. And Samuel said to Saul : Why hast thou disturbed my rest, that I should be brought up? And Saul said : I am in great distress : for the Philistines fight against me, and God is departed from me, and would not hear me, neither by the hand of prophets, nor by dreams : therefore I have called thee, that thou mayest shew me what I shall do. And Samuel said : Why askest thou me, seeing the Lord has departed from thee, and is gone over to thy rival? For the Lord will do to thee as He spoke by me, and He will rend thy kingdom out of thy hand, and will give it to thy neighbour David (1 *Kings* xxviii. 7).

Q. What other things are forbidden by this first commandment?

A. All charms, spells, and heathenish observations of omens, dreams, and such like fooleries.

And many of them who had followed curious arts, brought together their books, and burnt them before all : and counting the price of them, they found the money to be fifty thousand pieces of silver (*Acts* xix. 19).

Deceitful divinations and lying omens and the dreams of evil doers, are vanity (*Ecclus.* xxxiv. 5).

For dreams have deceived many, and they have failed that put their trust in them (*Ecclus.* xxxiv. 7).

Q. Does the first

He made also the propitiatory,

commandment forbid the making of images ?

A. The first commandment does not forbid the making of images, but the making of idols; that is, it forbids us to make images to be adored, or honoured as gods.

that is, the oracle, of the purest gold, two cubits and a half in length, and a cubit and a half in breadth. Two cherubim also of beaten gold, which he set on the two sides of the propitiatory : one cherub in the top of one side, and the other cherub in the top of the other side: two cherubim at the two ends of the propitiatory, spreading their wings and covering the propitiatory, and looking one towards the other, and towards it (*Exod.* xxxvii. 6).

And all the walls of the temple round about he carved with divers figures and carvings : and he made in them cherubim and palm-trees, and divers representations as it were standing out, and coming forth from the wall (3 *Kings* vi. 29).

He made also a molten sea of ten cubits from brim to brim, round all about, the height of it was five cubits, and a line of thirty cubits compassed it round about. And a graven work under the brim of it compassed it, for ten cubits going about the sea : there were two rows cast of chamfered sculptures. And it stood upon twelve oxen, of which three looked towards the north, and three towards the west, and three towards the south, and three towards the east, and the sea was above upon them, and their hinder parts were all hid within (3 *Kings* vii. 23).

And the Lord said to him : Make a brazen serpent, and set it up for a sign : whosoever being struck shall look on it, shall live. Moses therefore made a brazen serpent, and set it up for a sign : which when they that were bitten looked upon, they were healed (*Num.* xxi. 8).

Q. Is it forbidden to

Then Jesus saith to him : Begone,

give honour to the Saints and Angels?

A. It is forbidden to give them supreme or divine honour, for this belongs to God alone.

Q. Is it allowable to give them any kind of honour?

A. Yes; it is allowable to give them an inferior honour, for this is due to them, as the servants and special friends of God.

Q. And is it allowable to honour relics, crucifixes, and holy pictures?

A. Yes; with an inferior and relative honour, as they relate to Christ and His Saints, and are memorials of them.

Satan: for it is written, The Lord thy God shalt thou adore, and Him only shalt thou serve (*S. Matt.* iv. 10).

And I fell down before his feet, to adore him. And he saith to me: See thou do it not : I am thy fellow-servant, and of thy brethren who have the testimony of Jesus. Adore God (*Apoc.* xix. 10).

The just shall shine, and shall run to and fro like sparks among the reeds. They shall judge nations, and rule over people, and their Lord shall reign for ever (*Wisd.* iii. 7).

You are My friends; if you do the things that I command you. I will not now call you servants ; for the servant knoweth not what his lord doth. But I have called you friends : because all things whatsoever I have heard of My Father, I have made known to you (*S. John* xv. 14).

Then Peter answering, said to Him : Behold we have left all things, and have followed Thee: what therefore shall we have ? And Jesus said to them : Amen I say to you, that you, who have followed Me, in the regeneration, when the Son of Man shall sit on the seat of His majesty, you also shall sit on twelve seats judging the twelve tribes of Israel (*S. Matt.* xix. 27).

And he took up the mantle of Elias, that fell from him : and going back he stood upon the bank of the Jordan, and he struck the waters with the mantle of Elias, that had fallen from him, and they were not divided. And he said : Where is now the God of Elias? And he struck the waters, and they were divided, hither and thither, and

Eliseus passed over (4 *Kings* ii. 13).

And Eliseus died, and they buried him. And the rovers from Moab came into the land the same year. And some that were burying a man, saw the rovers, and cast the body into the sepulchre of Eliseus. And when it had touched the bones of Eliseus, the man came to life, and stood upon his feet (4 *Kings* xiii. 20).

And behold, a woman who was troubled with an issue of blood twelve years, came behind Him, and touched the hem of His garment. For she said within herself: If I shall touch only His garment, I shall be healed. But Jesus turning and seeing her, said: Be of good heart, daughter, thy faith hath made thee whole. And the woman was made whole from that hour (*S. Matt.* ix. 20).

And they besought Him that they might touch but the hem of His garment. And as many as touched, were made whole (*S. Matt.* xiv. 36).

And the multitude of men and women who believed in the Lord was more increased: insomuch that they brought forth the sick into the streets, and laid them on beds and couches, that when Peter came, his shadow at the least might overshadow any of them, and they might be delivered from their infirmities (*Acts* v. 14).

And God wrought by the hand of Paul more than common miracles. So that even there were brought from his body to the sick handkerchiefs and aprons, and the diseases departed from them, and the wicked spirits went out of them (*Acts* xix. 11).

Q. May we pray to relics or images?

The idols of the Gentiles are silver and gold, the works of the

A. No, by no means ; for they can neither see, nor hear, nor help us.

hands of men. They have mouths and speak not : they have eyes and see not. They have ears and hear not : they have noses and smell not. They have hands and feel not : they have feet and walk not : neither shall they cry out through their throat. Let them that make them become like unto them : and all such as trust in them (*Ps.* cxiii. 4, or cxiii. 12).

Q. What is the second commandment?

A. Thou shalt not take the Name of the Lord thy God in vain.

Thou shalt not take the Name of the Lord thy God in vain : for the Lord will not hold him guiltless that shall take the Name of the Lord his God in vain (*Exod.* xx. 7).

And let not the naming of God be usual in thy mouth, and meddle not with the names of saints, for thou shalt not escape free from them (*Ecclus.* xxiii. 10).

Q. What are we commanded by the second commandment?

A. We are commanded to speak with reverence of God and all holy things, and to keep our lawful oaths and vows.

If thou hast vowed any thing to God, defer not to pay it : for an unfaithful and foolish promise displeaseth Him : but whatsoever thou hast vowed, pay it. And it is much better not to vow, than after a vow not to perform the things promised (*Eccles.* v. 3).

Vow ye, and pay to the Lord your God (*Ps.* lxxv. 12).

Q. What does the second commandment forbid?

A. The second commandment forbids all false, rash, unjust, and unnecessary oaths ; as also blaspheming, cursing, and profane words.

But I say to you not to swear at all, neither by heaven, for it is the throne of God : nor by the earth, for it is His footstool : nor by Jerusalem, for it is the city of the Great King : neither shalt thou swear by thy head, because thou canst not make one hair white or black. But let your speech be yea, yea : no, no : and that which is over and above these, is of evil (*S. Matt.* v. 34).

But above all things, my brethren, swear not, neither by heaven nor by the earth, nor by any other oath.

But let your speech be, yea, yea : no, no : that you fall not under judgment (*S. James* v. 12).

Rash and unjust Oaths.

And when day was come, some of the Jews gathered together, and bound themselves under a curse, saying, that they would neither eat, nor drink, till they killed Paul (*Acts* xxiii. 12).

And he that blasphemeth the Name of the Lord, dying let him die : all the multitude shall stone him, whether he be a native or a stranger. He that blasphemeth the Name of the Lord, dying let him die (*Levit.* xxiv. 16).

But I say to you, that whosoever is angry with his brother, shall be in danger of the judgment. And whosoever shall say to his brother, Raca, shall be in danger of the council. And whosoever shall say, Thou fool, shall be in danger of hell fire (*S. Matt.* v. 22).

Q. What is the third commandment?

A. Remember that thou keep holy the Sabbath day.

Q. What are we commanded by the third commandment?

A. We are commanded to keep the Sunday holy.

Q. How are we to keep the Sunday holy?

A. By hearing Mass, and resting from servile works.

Keep you My sabbath : for it is holy unto you : he that shall profane it, shall be put to death : he that shall do any work in it, his soul shall perish out of the midst of his people. Six days shall you do work : in the seventh day is the sabbath, the rest holy to the Lord. Every one that shall do any work on this day, shall die. Let the children of Israel keep the sabbath, and celebrate it in their generations. It is an everlasting covenant (*Exod.* xxxi. 14).

For the Son of Man is Lord even of the Sabbath (*S. Matt.* xii. 8).

And on the first day of the week, when we were assembled to break bread, Paul discoursed with them, being to depart on the morrow (*Acts* xx. 7).

Q. Why are we commanded to rest from work?

A. That we may have time and opportunity for prayer, going to the Sacraments, hearing instructions, and reading good books.

Q. What does the third commandment forbid?

A. The third commandment forbids unnecessary servile work, and all profanation of the Lord's day.

And he said to them: The sabbath was made for man, and not man for the sabbath. Therefore the Son of Man is Lord of the sabbath also (*S. Mark* ii. 27).

Spirit of the Christian Sabbath.

And the ruler of the synagogue, (being angry that Jesus had healed on the sabbath) answering said to the multitude : Six days there are wherein you ought to work. In them therefore come, and be healed ; and not on the Sabbath-day. And the Lord answering him, said : Ye hypocrites, doth not every one of you on the Sabbath-day loose his ox or his ass from the manger, and lead them to water? And ought not this daughter of Abraham, whom Satan hath bound, lo, these eighteen years, be loosed from this bond on the Sabbath-day? (*S. Luke* xiii. 14.)

And answering them, He said : Which of you shall have an ass or an ox fall into a pit; and will not immediately draw him out on the Sabbath-day? (*S. Luke* xiv. 5.)

Or have ye not read in the law, that on the Sabbath-days the priests in the temple break the Sabbath, and are without blame? (*S. Matt.* xii. 5.)

Q. What is the fourth commandment?

A. Honour thy father and thy mother.

Honour thy father and thy mother, that thou mayest be long-lived upon the land which the Lord thy God will give thee (*Exod.* xx. 12).

Children, obey your parents in the Lord, for this is just. Honour thy father and thy mother, which is the first commandment with a promise : that it may be well with thee, and thou mayest be long-lived upon earth (*Eph.* vi. 1).

Q. What are we commanded by the fourth commandment?

A. We are commanded to love, honour, and obey our parents in all that is not sin.

Q. Are we commanded to obey our parents only?

A. No ; we must also obey our bishops, pastors, magistrates, and masters.

And he that honoureth his mother, is as one that layeth up a treasure. He that honoureth his father, shall have joy in his own children, and in the day of his prayer he shall be heard. He that honoureth his father, shall enjoy a long life : and he that obeyeth the father, shall be a comfort to his mother (*Ecclus.* iii. 5).

Children, obey your parents, in all things : for this is well pleasing to the Lord (*Col.* iii. 20).

Obedience to Pastors.

He that heareth you heareth Me ; and he that despiseth you despiseth Me ; and he that despiseth Me despiseth Him that sent Me (*S. Luke* x. 16).

Obey your prelates, and be subject to them. For they watch as being to render an account of your souls : that they may do this with joy, and not with grief. For this is not expedient for you (*Heb.* xiii. 17).

Obedience to Rulers and Masters.

Be ye subject therefore to every human creature for God's sake : whether it be to the king as excelling : or to governors as sent by Him for the punishment of evil doers, and for the praise of the good : for so is the will of God, that by doing well you may put to silence the ignorance of foolish men : as free, and not as making liberty a cloak for malice, but as the servants of God. Honour all men. Love the brotherhood. Fear God. Honour the king (1 *S. Pet.* ii. 13).

Servants, be subject to your masters with all fear, not only to the good and gentle, but also to the froward (1 *S. Pet.* ii. 18).

Servants, be obedient to them

that are your lords according to the flesh, with fear and trembling, in the simplicity of your heart as to Christ : not serving to the eye, as it were pleasing men, but as the servants of Christ, doing the will of God from the heart, with a good will serving, as to the Lord, and not to men. Knowing that whatsoever good thing any man shall do, the same shall he receive from the Lord, whether he be bond, or free (*Eph.* vi. 5).

Q. Are we bound to assist our parents in their wants ?

A. Yes, certainly ; both in their temporal and in their spiritual wants.

Q. Is it the duty of the faithful to contribute to the support of their pastors ?

A. Yes, it is just and commanded by Christ : for St. Paul says, " The Lord hath ordained that they who preach the Gospel should live by the Gospel " (1 *Cor.* ix. 14).

Know you not, that they who work in the holy place, eat the things that are of the holy place ; and they that serve the altar, partake with the altar? So also the Lord ordained that they who preached the gospel, should live by the gospel (1 *Cor.* ix. 13).

If we have sown unto you spiritual things, is it a great matter if we reap your carnal things ? (1 *Cor.* ix. 11.)

Who serveth as a soldier at any time, at his own charges? Who planteth a vineyard, and eateth not of the fruit thereof? Who feedeth a flock, and eateth not of the milk of the flock ? (1 *Cor.* ix. 7.)

And in the same house remain, eating and drinking such things as they have. For the labourer is worthy of his hire. Remove not from house to house. And into what city soever you enter, and they receive you, eat such things as are set before you (*S. Luke* x. 7).

Q. And what is the duty of parents and of other superiors?

A. To take proper care of all under their charge, and to bring up their children in the fear of God.

And you fathers, provoke not your children to anger: but bring them up in the discipline and correction of the Lord (*Eph.* vi. 4).

And you masters, do the same things to them, forbearing threatenings: knowing, that the Lord both of them and you is in Heaven : and there is no respect of persons with Him (*Eph.* vi. 9).

Masters, do to your servants that which is just and equal, knowing that you also have a Master in Heaven (*Col.* iv. 1).

For I have foretold unto him, that I will judge his house for ever, for iniquity, because he knew that his sons did wickedly, and did not chastise them (1 *Kings* iii. 13).

A foolish son is the anger of the father: and the sorrow of the mother that bore him (*Prov.* xvii. 25).

A son ill taught is the confusion of the father : and a foolish daughter shall be to his loss (*Ecclus.* xxii. 3).

Q. What does the fourth commandment forbid?

A. The fourth commandment forbids all contempt, stubbornness, and disobedience to our parents and lawful superiors.

If a man have a stubborn and unruly son, who will not hear the commandments of his father or mother, and being corrected, slighteth obedience : they shall take him and bring him to the ancients of his city, and to the gate of judgment, and shall say to them: This our son is rebellious and stubborn, he slighteth hearing our admonitions, he giveth himself to revelling, and to debauchery and banquetings : the people of the city shall stone him : and he shall die, that you may take away the evil out of the midst of you, and all Israel hearing it may be afraid (*Deut.* xxi. 18).

He that curseth his father, and mother, his lamp shall be put out in the midst of darkness (*Prov.* xx. 20).

Q. What is the fifth commandment?

A. Thou shalt not kill.

Q. What does the fifth commandment forbid?

A. The fifth commandment forbids all wilful murder, fighting, quarrelling, and injurious words.

And the Lord said to Cain: Where is thy brother Abel? And he answered, I know not: am I my brother's keeper? And He said to him: What hast thou done? the voice of thy brother's blood crieth to Me from the earth. Now, therefore, cursed shalt thou be upon the earth, which hath opened her mouth and received the blood of thy brother at thy hand (*Gen.* iv. 9).

Whosoever shall shed man's blood, his blood shall be shed: for man was made to the image of God (*Gen.* ix. 6).

He that striketh, and killeth a man, dying let him die (*Levit.* xxiv. 17).

As the vapour of a chimney, and the smoke of the fire goeth up before the fire: so also injurious words, and reproaches, and threats, before blood (*Ecclus.* xxii. 30).

Q. Does it forbid anger?

A. Yes; as also hatred and revenge.

Be angry, and sin not. Let not the sun go down upon your anger. Give not place to the devil (*Eph.* iv. 26).

You know, my dearest brethren. And let every man be swift to hear, but slow to speak, and slow to anger. For the anger of man worketh not the justice of God (*S. James* i. 19).

Whosoever hateth his brother, is a murderer. And you know that no murderer hath eternal life abiding in himself (1 *S. John* iii. 15).

If it be possible, as much as is in you, having peace with all men. Not revenging yourselves, my dearly beloved; but give place unto wrath, for it is written: Revenge to Me: I will repay, saith the Lord. But if thy enemy be hungry, give him to eat: if he thirst, give him to drink. For, doing this, thou shalt heap coals of fire upon his head. Be not overcome by evil, but overcome evil by good (*Rom.* xii. 18).

He that seeketh to revenge himself, shall find vengeance from the Lord, and He will surely keep his sins in remembrance (*Ecclus.*xxviii.1).

Then his lord called him ; and said to him : Thou wicked servant, I forgave thee all the debt, because thou besoughtest me : shouldst not thou then have had compassion also on thy fellow-servant, even as I had compassion on thee? And his lord being angry, delivered him to the torturers until he should pay all the debt. So also shall My heavenly Father do to you, if you forgive not every one his brother from your hearts (*S. Matt.* xviii. 32).

If therefore thou offer thy gift at the altar, and there thou remember that thy brother hath any thing against thee ; leave there thy offering before the altar, and go first to be reconciled to thy brother: and then coming thou shalt offer thy gift (*S. Matt.* v. 23).

Thou shalt not hate thy brother in thy heart, but reprove him openly, lest thou incur sin through him. Seek not revenge, nor be mindful of the injury of thy citizens. Thou shalt love thy friend as thyself. I am the Lord (*Levit.* xix. 17).

Q. What else is forbidden by the fifth commandment?

A. Giving scandal, and bad example.

But he that shall scandalize one of these little ones that believe in Me, it were better for him that a millstone should be hanged about his neck, and that he should be drowned in the depth of the sea. Woe to the world because of scandals. For it must needs be that scandals come: but nevertheless woe to that man by whom the scandal cometh (*S. Matt.* xviii. 6).

And if thy right eye scandalize

thee, pluck it out and cast it from thee. For it is expedient for thee that one of thy members should perish, rather than thy whole body be cast into hell. And if thy right hand scandalize thee, cut it off, and cast it from thee; for it is expedient for thee that one of thy members should perish, rather than that thy whole body go into hell (*S. Matt.* v. 29).

And through thy knowledge shall the weak brother perish, for whom Christ hath died? Now when you sin thus against the brethren, and wound their weak conscience, you sin against Christ. Wherefore if meat scandalize my brother, I will never eat flesh, lest I should scandalize my brother (1 *Cor.* viii. 11).

Q. What is the sixth commandment?

A. Thou shalt not commit adultery.

Q. What does the sixth commandment forbid?

A. The sixth commandment forbids all sins of uncleanness with another's wife or husband.

Q. What else is forbidden by the sixth commandment?

A. All other kinds of immodesties, by kisses, touches, looks, words, or actions.

Q. What ought we to think of immodest plays and dances?

A. They are also for-

If any man commit adultery with the wife of another, and defile his neighbour's wife, let them be put to death, both the adulterer and the adulteress (*Levit.* xx. 10).

Mortify therefore your members which are upon the earth, fornication, uncleanness, lust, evil concupiscence, and covetousness, which is the service of idols. For which things the wrath of God cometh upon the children of unbelief (*Col.* iii. 5).

But fornication and all uncleanness, or covetousness, let it not so much as be named among you, as becometh saints. Or obscenity, or foolish talking, or scurrility, which is to no purpose: but rather giving of thanks (*Eph.* v. 3).

I made a covenant with my eyes, that I would not so much as think upon a virgin. For what part should God from above have in me, and what inheritance the Almighty from on high? (*Job* xxxi. 1.)

bidden by this commandment; and it is sinful to be present at them.

Q. Does this commandment forbid us to read immodest books?
A. Yes ; for such reading is very dangerous, and generally sinful.

Gaze not upon a maiden, lest her beauty be a stumbling-block to thee (*Ecclus.* ix. 5).

For from the heart come forth evil thoughts, murders, adulteries, fornications, thefts, false testimonies, blasphemies. These are the things that defile a man (*S. Matt.* xv. 19).

Blessed are the clean of heart: for they shall see God (*S. Matt.* v. 8).

O how beautiful is the chaste generation with glory: for the memory thereof is immortal: because it is known both with God and with men. When it is present, they imitate it: and they desire it when it hath withdrawn itself, and it triumpheth crowned for ever, winning the reward of undefiled conflicts (*Wisd.* iv. 1).

Be not deceived; God is not mocked: for whatsoever a man soweth, that shall he also reap. For he that soweth to his flesh shall of the flesh reap corruption; but he that soweth to the Spirit shall of the Spirit reap life everlasting (*Gal.* vi. 7).

Q. What is the seventh commandment?
A. Thou shalt not steal.

Q. What does the seventh commandment forbid?
A. The seventh commandment forbids all unjust taking away, or keeping what belongs to another.

He that stole, let him now steal no more, but rather let him labour working with his hands the thing which is good, that he may have something to give to him that suffereth need (*Eph.* iv. 28).

But let none of you suffer as a murderer, or a thief, or a railer, or a coveter of other men's things. But if as a Christian, let him not be ashamed, but let him glorify God in this name (1 *S. Pet.* iv. 15).

Render therefore to all men their dues. Tribute, to whom tribute is due: custom to whom custom: fear to whom fear: honour to whom honour (*Rom.* xiii. 7).

Q. What else is forbidden by the seventh commandment?

A. All manner of cheating in buying and selling; or any other way of wronging our neighbour.

Q. Must we restore ill-gotten goods?

A. Yes, if we are able, or else the sin will not be forgiven: we must also pay our debts.

Q. What is the eighth commandment?

A. Thou shalt not bear false witness against thy neighbour.

Q. What does the eighth commandment forbid?

A. The eighth commandment forbids all false testimony, rash judgment, and lies.

A deceitful balance is an abomination before the Lord : and a just weight is His will (*Prov.* xi. 1). '

Diverse weights are an abomination before the Lord : a deceitful balance is not good (*Prov.* xx. 23).

But Zacheus standing said to the Lord, Behold, Lord, the half of my goods I give to the poor: and if I have wronged any man of any thing, I restore him four-fold. Jesus said to him: This day is salvation come to this house, because he also is a son of Abraham (*S. Luke* xix. 8).

And bringing two men sons of the devil, they made them sit against him : and they, like men of the devil, bore witness against him before the people, saying: Naboth hath blasphemed God and the king : wherefore they brought him forth without the city, and stoned him to death. And they sent to Jezabel, saying : Naboth is stoned, and is dead (3 *Kings* xxi. 13).

Rash Judgment.

Who art thou that judgest another man's servant ? To his own lord he standeth or falleth. And he shall stand; for God is able to make him stand (*Rom.* xiv. 4).

Judge not, and you shall not be judged. Condemn not, and you shall not be condemned. Forgive, and you shall be forgiven (*S. Luke* vi. 37).

Lying.

There shall not enter into it any thing defiled, or that worketh abomination and maketh a lie, but they that are written in the book of life of the Lamb (*Apoc.* xxi. 27).

A lie is a foul blot in a man, and yet it will be continually in the mouth of men without discipline. A thief is better than a man that is always lying : but both of them shall inherit destruction (*Ecclus.* xx. 26).

Lying lips are an abomination to the Lord : but they that deal faithfully please Him (*Prov.* xii. 22).

Hypocrisy.

And when great multitudes stood about Him, so that they trod one upon another, He began to say to His disciples : Beware ye of the leaven of the Pharisees, which is hypocrisy (*S. Luke* xii. 1).

Therefore let us feast, not with the old leaven, nor with the leaven of malice and wickedness, but with the unleavened bread of sincerity and truth (1 *Cor.* v. 8).

Q. What else is forbidden by the eighth commandment?

A. All calumny, detraction, and backbiting, or any words which injure our neighbour's character.

Lying lips hide hatred : he that uttereth reproach is foolish. In the multitude of words there shall not want sin : but he that refraineth his lips is most wise (*Prov.* x. 18).

The man that in private detracted his neighbour, him did I persecute. With him that had a proud eye, and an unsatiable heart, I would not eat (*Ps.* c. 5).

Q. What is he bound to do who has injured his neighbour by speaking ill of him?

A. He must make him satisfaction, and restore his good name as far as he is able.

Q. What is the ninth commandment?

A. Thou shalt not covet thy neighbour's wife?

Q. What does the ninth commandment forbid?

A. The ninth commandment forbids all lustful thoughts and desires, and all wilful pleasure in the irregular motions of the flesh.

Q. What is the tenth commandment?

A. Thou shalt not covet thy neighbour's goods.

Q. What does the tenth commandment forbid?

A. The tenth commandment forbids all covetous thoughts and unjust desires of our neighbour's goods and profits.

But every man is tempted by his own concupiscence, being drawn away and allured. Then when concupiscence hath conceived, it bringeth forth sin. But sin, when it is completed, begetteth death (*S. James* i. 14).

You have heard that it was said to them of old : Thou shalt not commit adultery. But I say to you, that whosoever shall look on a woman to lust after her, hath already committed adultery with her in his heart (*S. Matt.* v. 27).

For all that is in the world is the concupiscence of the flesh, and the concupiscence of the eyes, and the pride of life, which is not of the Father, but is of the world. And the world passeth away, and the concupiscence thereof (1 *S. John* ii. 16).

CHAPTER V.

THE COMMANDMENTS OF THE CHURCH.

Q. Are we bound to obey the Church?

A. Yes; because Christ has said to the

pastors of the Church, " He that heareth you, heareth Me ; and he that depiseth you, despiseth Me " (*Luke* x. 16).

Q. Which are the chief commandments of the Church ?

A. 1. To keep certain days holy, with the obligation of resting from servile works.

2. To hear Mass on all Sundays and Holy-days of obligation.

3. To keep the days of fasting and abstinence appointed by the Church.

4. To go to confession at least once a year.

5. To receive the Blessed Sacrament at least once a year, and that at Easter or there-abouts.

6. Not to marry within certain degrees of kindred, nor to solemnize marriage at the forbidden times.

Q. What is the first commandment of the Church ?

A. To keep certain days holy, with the obligation of resting from servile works.

Q. What are these days called ?

A. They are called Holy-days of obligation.

Q. What is the second

commandment of the Church?

A. To hear Mass on all Sundays and Holydays of obligation.

Q. What is the third commandment of the Church?

A. To keep the days of fasting and abstinence appointed by the Church.

Q. What is meant by fasting days?

A. Days on which we are allowed to take but one meal, and are forbidden to eat flesh meat.

Q. Which are the fasting days?

A. The forty days of Lent; certain Vigils; the Ember days; and in England the Wednesdays and Fridays of Advent.

Q. What is meant by days of abstinence?

A. Days on which we are forbidden to eat flesh meat, but are allowed the usual number of meals.

Q. Which are days of abstinence?

A. All Fridays, except the Friday on which Christmas-day may fall; and the Sundays in Lent, unless leave be given to eat meat on them.

Then was Jesus led up by the spirit into the wilderness to be tempted by the deviL And when He had fasted forty days and forty nights, He was afterward hungry (*S. Matt.* iv. 1).

And when you fast, be not as the hypocrites, sad. For they disfigure their faces, that they may appear unto men to fast. Amen I say to you, they have received their reward. But thou, when thou fastest, anoint thy head, and wash thy face; that thou appear not to men to fast, but to thy Father who is in secret: and thy Father who seeth in secret, will repay thee (*S. Matt.* vi. 16).

And the disciples of John and the Pharisees used to fast: and they come and say to Him: Why do the disciples of John and of the Pharisees fast; but Thy disciples do not fast? And Jesus saith to them : Can the children of the marriage fast, as long as the bridegroom is with them? As long as they have the bridegroom with them, they cannot fast. But the days will come when the bridegroom shall be taken away from them : and then they shall fast in those days (*S. Mark* ii. 18).

But this kind is not cast out but by prayer and fasting (*S. Matt.* xvii. 20).

Now therefore saith the Lord : Be converted to Me with all your heart, in fasting, and in weeping, and in mourning. And rend your hearts, and not your garments, and turn to the Lord our God : for He is gracious and merciful, patient and rich in mercy, and ready to repent of the evil (*Joel* ii. 12).

Why have we fasted, and Thou hast not regarded : have we humbled our souls, and Thou hast not taken notice ? Behold in the day of your fast your own will is found, and you exact of all your debtors (*Isa.* lviii. 3).

Then they fasting and praying, and imposing their hands upon them, sent them away (*Acts* xiii. 3).

Eleazar one of the chief of the scribes, a man advanced in years, and of a comely countenance, was pressed to open his mouth to eat swine's flesh. But he, choosing rather a most glorious death than a hateful life, went forward voluntarily to the torment. And considering in what manner he was to come to it, patiently bearing, he determined not to do any unlawful things for the love of life (2 *Mach.* vi. 18).

Q. Why does the Church command us to fast and abstain ?

A. That so we may mortify the flesh and satisfy God for our sins.

And He said to all : If any man will come after Me, let him deny himself, and take up his cross daily, and follow Me (*S. Luke* ix. 23).

Strive to enter by the narrow gate : for many, I say unto you, shall seek to enter, and shall not be able (*S. Luke* xiii. 24).

And every one that striveth for the mastery refraineth himself from all things : and they indeed that they may receive a corruptible crown ; but we an incorruptible one. I therefore so run, not as at any uncertainty : I so fight, not as one beating the air : but I chastise my body, and bring it into subjection : lest perhaps, when I have preached to others, I myself should become a cast-away (1 *Cor.* ix. 25).

And from the days of John the Baptist until now, the kingdom of heaven suffereth violence, and the violent bear it away (*S. Matt.* xi. 12).

Q. What is the fourth commandment of the Church?

A. To go to confession at least once a year.

Q. How soon are children bound to go to confession?

A. As soon as they come to the use of reason, so as to be capable of mortal sin.

Q. When are children generally supposed to come to the use of reason?

A. About the age of seven years.

Q. What is the fifth commandment of the Church?

A. To receive the Blessed Sacrament at least once a year, and that at Easter or thereabouts.

Q. How soon are Christians bound to receive the Blessed Sacrament?

A. As soon as they are capable of being instructed in that sacred mystery.

Q. What is the sixth commandment of the Church?

A. Not to marry within certain degrees of kindred, nor to solemnize marriage at the forbidden times.

Q. Which are those forbidden times?
A. From the first Sunday of Advent till after the Epiphany, and from Ash Wednesday till after Low Sunday.

CHAPTER VI.

THE SACRAMENTS.

Q. What is a sacrament?
A. A sacrament is an outward sign of inward grace, ordained by Christ, by which grace is given to our souls.

Q. Do the sacraments always give grace?
A. Yes; to those who receive them worthily.

Q. Whence have the sacraments the power of giving grace?
A. From the merits of Christ's Precious Blood, which they apply to our souls.

But if we walk in the light, as He also is in the light: we have fellowship one with another, and the blood of Jesus Christ His Son cleanseth us from all sin (1 *S. John* i. 7).

And to Jesus the Mediator of the New Testament, and to the sprinkling of blood which speaketh better than that of Abel (*Heb.* xii. 24).

Wherefore Jesus also, that He might sanctify the people by His own blood, suffered without the gate. Let us go forth therefore to Him without the camp; bearing His reproach (*Heb.* xiii. 12).

These are they who are come out of great tribulation, and have washed their robes, and have made them white in the blood of the Lamb (*Apoc.* vii. 14).

And they sung a new canticle, saying: Thou art worthy, O Lord, to take the book, and to open the seals thereof: because Thou wast slain, and hast redeemed us to God, in Thy blood, out of every tribe, and tongue, and people, and nation (*Apoc.* v. 9).

Q. Is it a great happiness to receive the sacraments worthily?

A. Yes; it is the greatest happiness in the world.

Many waters cannot quench charity, neither can the floods drown it: if a man should give all the substance of his house for love, he shall despise it as nothing (*Cant.* viii. 7).

Q. How many sacraments are there?

A. These seven: Baptism, Confirmation, Holy Eucharist, Penance, Extreme Unction, Holy Order, and Matrimony.

Q. What is Baptism?

A. Baptism is a sacrament by which we are made Christians, children of God, and members of the Church.

Go ye therefore, and teach all nations, baptizing them in the Name of the Father, and of the Son, and of the Holy Ghost (*S. Matt.* xxviii. 19).

And as they went on their way, they came to a certain water: and the eunuch said: See here is water, what doth hinder me from being baptized? And Philip said: If thou believest with all thy heart thou mayst. And he answering, said: I believe that Jesus Christ is the

Son of God. And he commanded the chariot to stand still: and they went down into the water, both Philip and the eunuch, and he baptized him (*Acts* viii. 36).

One Lord, one faith, one baptism (*Eph.* iv. 5).

For as many of you as have been baptized in Christ, have put on Christ (*Gal.* iii. 27).

Q. What other grace is given by this sacrament?

A. It cleanses us from original sin, and also from actual, if we be guilty of any.

Now when they had heard these things, they had compunction in their heart, and said to Peter, and to the rest of the apostles: What shall we do, men and brethren? But Peter said to them: Do penance, and be baptized every one of you, in the Name of Jesus Christ, for the remission of your sins: and you shall receive the gift of the Holy Ghost (*Acts* ii. 37).

And now why tarriest thou? Rise up, and be baptized, and wash away thy sins, invoking His Name (*Acts* xxii. 16).

Q. Can no one but a Priest baptize?

A. In case of necessity, when a Priest cannot be had, any one may baptize.

He that believeth and is baptized, shall be saved: but he that believeth not, shall be condemned (*S. Mark* xvi. 16).

In which also coming He preached to those spirits that were in prison: which had been some time incredulous, when they waited for the patience of God in the days of Noe, when the ark was a building: wherein a few, that is, eight souls, were saved by water. Whereunto baptism being of the like form, now saveth you also: not the putting away of the filth of the flesh, but the examination of a good conscience towards God by the resurrection of Jesus Christ (1 *S. Pet.* iii. 19).

Q. How is Baptism given?

A. By pouring water on the head of the child, whilst we pronounce the words ordained by Christ.

Q. What are those words?

A. "I baptize thee, in the Name of the Father, and of the

And he said to them: Have you received the Holy Ghost since ye

Son, and of the Holy
Ghost."

Q. What do we pro-
mise in Baptism?
A. To renounce the
devil, and all his works
and pomps.

Q. Is Baptism neces-
sary for salvation?
A. Yes; for Christ
says: "Unless a man be
born again of water and
the Holy Ghost, he can-
not enter the kingdom
of God "(*John* iii. 5).

Q. What is Confirma-
tion?
A. Confirmation is a
sacrament by which we
receive the Holy Ghost,
in order to make us
strong and perfect Chris-
tians and soldiers of
Jesus Christ.

believed? But they said to him:
We have not so much as heard
whether there be a Holy Ghost.
And he said: In what then were
you baptized? Who said: In John's
baptism. Then Paul said: John
baptized the people with the baptism of penance, saying: That they
should believe in Him who was to
come after him, that is to say, in
Jesus. Having heard these things,
they were baptized in the Name of
the Lord Jesus (*Acts* xix. 2).

And I will ask the Father, and
He shall give you another Paraclete,
that He may abide with you for ever
(*S. John* xiv. 16).

But the Paraclete, the Holy Ghost,
whom the Father will send in My
Name, He will teach you all things,
and bring all things to your mind,
whatsoever I shall have said to you
(*S. John* xiv. 26).

And when the days of the pentecost were accomplished, they were all
together in one place: and suddenly there came a sound from
heaven, as of a mighty wind coming,
and it filled the whole house where
they were sitting. And there appeared
to them parted tongues as it were of
fire, and it sat upon every one of
them: and they were all filled with
the Holy Ghost, and they began to
speak with divers tongues, according
as the Holy Ghost gave them to
speak (*Acts* ii. 1).

Wherefore leaving the word of
the beginning of Christ, let us go
on to things more perfect, not lay-
ing again the foundation of penance
from dead works, and of faith to-

wards God, of the doctrine of baptisms, and imposition of hands, and of the resurrection of the dead, and of eternal judgment (*Heb.* vi. 1).

And the spirit of the Lord shall rest upon him: the spirit of wisdom, and of understanding, the spirit of counsel, and of fortitude, the spirit of knowledge, and of godliness. And he shall be filled with the spirit of the fear of the Lord. He shall not judge according to the sight of the eyes, nor reprove according to the hearing of the ears (*Isa.* xi. 2).

But the fruit of the Spirit is, charity, joy, peace, patience, benignity, goodness, longanimity, mildness, faith, modesty, continency, chastity. Against such there is no law (*Gal.* v. 22).

Q. Who is the ordinary minister of Confirmation?

A. A Bishop only.

Now when the apostles who were in Jerusalem, had heard that Samaria had received the word of God; they sent unto them Peter and John. Who when they were come, prayed for them, that they might receive the Holy Ghost. For He was not as yet come upon any of them : but they were only baptized in the Name of the Lord Jesus (*Acts* viii. 14).

Q. How does the Bishop administer this sacrament?

A. He prays that the Holy Ghost may come down upon us; he imposes his hands on us, making the sign of the Cross with chrism on our forehead, at the same time pronouncing a set form of words.

Then they laid their hands upon them, and they received the Holy Ghost (*Acts* viii. 17).

Q. What are those words?

A. "I sign thee with the sign of the Cross, and I confirm thee with the chrism of salvation, in the name of the Father, and of the Son, and of the Holy Ghost."

Q. What is the Holy Eucharist [1]?

A. It is the true body and blood of Christ, under the appearances of bread and wine.

Q. How are the bread and wine changed into the body and blood of Christ?

A. By the power of God, to whom nothing is impossible or difficult.

Use of Holy Oil.

Thou shalt anoint Aaron and his sons, and shalt sanctify them, that they may do the office of priesthood unto Me. And thou shalt say to the children of Israel: This oil of unction shall be holy unto Me throughout your generations. The flesh of man shall not be anointed therewith, and you shall make none other of the same composition, because it is sanctified, and shall be holy unto you (*Exod.* xxx. 30).

Promise.

I am the living bread, which came down from heaven. If any man eat of this bread, he shall live for ever: and the bread that I will give, is My flesh for the life of the world. The Jews therefore strove among themselves, saying: How can this man give us His flesh to eat? Then Jesus said to them: Amen, amen, I say unto you: Except you eat the flesh of the Son of Man, and drink His blood, you shall not have life in you. He that eateth My flesh, and drinketh My blood, hath everlasting life: and I will raise him up in the last day. For My flesh is meat indeed: and My blood is drink indeed (*S. John* vi. 51).

Institution.

And whilst they were at supper, Jesus took bread, and blessed, and broke: and gave to his disciples, and said: Take ye, and eat: this is My body. And taking the chalice He gave thanks: and gave to them, saying: Drink ye all of this. For this is My blood of the new testament which shall be shed for many

[1] See note C, on the Real Presence.

unto remission of sins (*S. Matt.* xxvi. 26).

Subsequent References.

For I have received of the Lord that which also I delivered unto you, that the Lord Jesus, the same night in which he was betrayed, took bread, and giving thanks, broke, and said : Take ye and eat : this is My body which shall be delivered for you : this do for the commemoration of Me. In like manner also the chalice, after he had supped, saying : This chalice is the new testament in My blood : this do ye, as often as you shall drink, for the commemoration of Me. For as often as you shall eat this bread, and drink the chalice, you shall shew the death of the Lord until He come. Therefore whosoever shall eat this bread, or drink the chalice of the Lord unworthily, shall be guilty of the body and of the blood of the Lord (1 *Cor.* xi. 23).

The chalice of benediction, which we bless, is it not the communion of the blood of Christ? And the bread, which we break, is it not the partaking of the body of the Lord ? (1 *Cor.* x. 16.)

Miracles Illustrating the Miracle of Transubstantiation.

Q. When is this change made ?

A. When the words of consecration ordained by Jesus Christ are pronounced by the Priest in the Mass.

Jesus saith to them : Fill the water-pots with water. And they filled them up to the brim. And Jesus saith to them : Draw out now, and carry to the chief steward of the feast. And they carried it. And when the chief steward had tasted the water made wine, and knew not whence it was, but the waiters knew who had drawn the water (*S. John* ii. 7).

And Jesus took the loaves : and

when He had given thanks, He distributed to them that were sat down. In like manner also of the fishes as much as they would. And when they were filled, He said to His disciples : Gather up the fragments that remain, lest they be lost. They gathered up therefore, and filled twelve baskets with the fragments of the five barley loaves, which remained over and above to them that had eaten (*S. John* vi. 11).

Institution of the Holy Eucharist.

And taking bread, He gave thanks, and brake : and gave to them, saying : This is My body which is given for you. Do this for a commemoration of Me. In like manner the chalice also, after He had supped, saying : This is the chalice, the new testament in My blood, which shall be shed for you (*S. Luke* xxii. 19).

Figures of the Holy Eucharist.

Q. Why has Christ given Himself to us in this sacrament ?

A. To feed and nourish our souls, that we may live by Him.

And He said : Behold Adam is become as one of us, knowing good and evil : now, therefore, lest perhaps he put forth his hand, and take also of the tree of life, and eat, and live for ever (*Gen.* iii. 22).

And the Angel of the Lord came again the second time, and touched him, and said to him : Arise, eat : for thou hast yet a great way to go. And he arose, and ate, and drank, and walked in the strength of that food forty days and forty nights, unto the mount of God, Horeb (3 *Kings* xix. 8).

Our fathers did eat manna in the desert, as it is written : He gave them bread from heaven to eat. Then Jesus said to them : Amen, amen, I say to you : Moses gave you not bread from heaven, but My Father giveth you the true bread from heaven. For the bread of God is that which cometh down from heaven, and giveth life to the world (*S. John* vi. 31).

Promises.

I am the vine ; you the branches: he that abideth in Me, and I in him, the same beareth much fruit : for without Me you can do nothing. If any one abide not in Me : he shall be cast forth as a branch, and shall wither, and they shall gather him up, and cast him into the fire, and he burneth (*S. John* xv. 5).

He that eateth My flesh, and drinketh My blood, abideth in Me, and I in him. As the living Father hath sent Me, and I live by the Father : so he that eateth Me, the same also shall live by Me. This is the bread that came down from heaven. Not as your fathers did eat manna, and are dead. He that eateth this bread shall live for ever (*S. John* vi. 57).

He that hath an ear, let him hear what the Spirit saith to the churches : To him that overcometh, I will give the hidden manna, and will give him a white counter, and in the counter a new name written, which no man knoweth, but he that receiveth it (*Apoc.* ii. 17).

And He had commanded the clouds from above, and had opened the doors of heaven. And had rained down manna upon them to eat, and had given them the bread of heaven. Man ate the bread of angels : He sent them provisions in abundance (*Ps.* lxxvii. 23).

Instead of which things thou didst feed thy people with the food of angels, and gavest them bread from heaven prepared without labour ; having in it all that is delicious, and

the sweetness of every taste. For
thy sustenance shewed thy sweetness
to thy children, and serving every
man's will, it was turned to what
every man liked (*Wisd.* xvi. 20).

Neither is there any other nation
.so great, that hath gods so nigh
them, as our God is present to all
our petitions (*Deut.* iv. 7).

Jesus answered, and said to her :
Whosoever drinketh of this water,
shall thirst again ; but he that shall
drink of the water that I will give
him, shall not thirst for ever : but
the water that I will give him, shall
become in him a fountain of water
springing up into life everlasting (*S.
John* iv. 13).

And they told what things were
done in the way : and how they
knew Him in the breaking of bread
(*S. Luke* xxiv. 35).

The Wedding Garment of Grace.

And the king went in to see the
guests : and he saw there a man who
had not on a wedding garment. And
he saith to him : Friend, how camest
thou in hither not having a wedding
garment? But he was silent. Then
the king said to the waiters : Bind
his hands and feet, and cast him
into the exterior darkness : there
shall be weeping and gnashing of
teeth (*S. Matt.* xxii. 11).

Necessity of Preparation.

But let a man prove himself : and
so let him eat of that bread, and
drink of the chalice (1 *Cor.* xi. 28).

But if we should judge ourselves,
we would not be judged (1 *Cor.* xi. 31).

Jesus answered, and said to him :
If any man love Me, he will keep
My word, and My Father will love
him, and we will come to him,
and will make our abode with him
(*S. John* xiv. 23).

Q. What is required
of us before we receive
the Blessed Sacrament ?
A. We must be in a
state of grace ; we must
also be fasting from
midnight.

And when Jesus was come to the place, looking up, He saw him, and said to him : Zacheus, make haste and come down : for this day I must abide in thy house. And he made haste and came down, and received Him with joy(*S. Luke* xix. 5).

Q. Is it a great sin to receive unworthily?
A. Yes, it is ; "for he that eateth and drinketh unworthily, eateth and drinketh judgment to himself" (1 *Cor.* xi. 29).

Jesus answered: He it is to whom I shall reach bread dipped. And when He had dipped the bread, He gave it to Judas Iscariot, the son of Simon. And after the morsel, Satan entered into him. And Jesus said to him : That which thou dost, do quickly (*S. John* xiii. 26).

For he that eateth and drinketh unworthily, eateth and drinketh judgment to himself, not discerning the body of the Lord. Therefore are there many infirm and weak among you, and many sleep (1 *Cor.* xi. 29).

Q. What is meant by receiving unworthily?
A. Receiving in mortal sin.

Peter saith to Him : Thou shalt never wash my feet. Jesus answered him : If I wash thee not, thou shalt have no part with Me. Simon Peter saith to Him : Lord, not only my feet, but also my hands and my head (*S. John* xiii. 8).

And Azarias the high-priest, and all the rest of the priests looked upon him, and saw the leprosy in his forehead, and they made haste to thrust him out. Yea, himself also being frightened, hasted to go out, because he had quickly felt the stroke of the Lord (2 *Paral.* xxvi. 20).

Christ a Continual Sacrifice.

Q. Is the Blessed Eucharist a sacrament only?
A. No ; it is also a sacrifice.

Q. What is this sacrifice called?

And power was given Him over every tribe, and people, and tongue, and nation. And all that dwell upon the earth adored Him, whose names are not written in the book of life of the Lamb, which was slain from the beginning of the world (*Apoc.* xiii. 7).

A. It is called the Sacrifice of the Mass.

And I saw: and behold in the midst of the throne and of the four living creatures, and in the midst of the ancients, a Lamb standing as it were slain, having seven horns and seven eyes: which are the seven Spirits of God, sent forth into all the earth (*Apoc.* v. 6).

But Christ, being come an high-priest of the good things to come, by a greater and more perfect tabernacle not made with hand, that is, not of this creation: neither by the blood of goats, or of calves, but by His own blood, entered once into the Holies, having obtained eternal redemption. For if the blood of goats and of oxen, and the ashes of an heifer being sprinkled, sanctify such as are defiled, to the cleansing of the flesh: how much more shall the blood of Christ, who by the Holy Ghost offered Himself unspotted unto God, cleanse our conscience from dead works, to serve the living God? And therefore He is the Mediator of the new testament: that by means of His death, for the redemption of those transgressions, which were under the former testament, they that are called may receive the promise of eternal inheritance (*Heb.* ix. 11).

And they were persevering in the doctrine of the Apostles, and in the communication of the breaking of bread, and in prayers (*Acts* ii. 42).

Q. What, then, is the Mass?

A. It is the unbloody sacrifice of the Body and Blood of Christ [a].

For he testifieth: Thou art a priest for ever, according to the order of Melchisedech (*Heb.* vii. 17).

And the others indeed were made many priests, because by reason of death they were not suffered to continue: but this, that He continueth for ever, hath an everlasting priesthood.

[a] See note D, the Ancient Liturgies on the Real Presence.

Whereby He is able also to save for ever them that come to God by Him : always living to make intercession for us. For it was fitting that we should have such a high-priest, holy, innocent, undefiled, separated from sinners, and made higher than the heavens : who needeth not daily (as the other priests) to offer sacrifices first for His own sins, and then for the people's : for this He did once, in offering Himself (*Heb.* vii. 23).

Purge out the old leaven, that you may be a new paste, as you are un-leavened. For Christ our pasch, is sacrificed (1 *Cor.* v. 7).

Q. What are the ends for which this sacrifice is offered ?

A. First. For God's honour and glory. Secondly. As a thanksgiving for all His benefits. Thirdly. For obtaining pardon of our sins. And fourthly. For obtaining all graces and blessings through Jesus Christ.

And it came to pass after many days, that Cain offered, of the fruits of the earth, gifts to the Lord. Abel also offered of the firstlings of his flock, and of their fat (*Gen.* iv. 3).

And Noe built an altar unto the Lord : and taking of all cattle and fowls that were clean, offered holo-causts upon the altar. And the Lord smelled a sweet savour, and said : I will no more curse the earth for the sake of man : for the imagination and thought of man's heart are prone to evil from his youth : therefore I will no more destroy every living soul as I have done (*Gen.* viii. 20).

But Melchisedech, the king of Salem, bringing forth bread and wine, for he was the priest of the Most High God, blessed him, and said : Blessed be Abram by the Most High God, who created heaven and earth (*Gen.* xiv. 18).

And Abraham said : God will provide Himself a victim for a holo-caust, my son. So they went on together. And they came to the place which God had shewn him, where he built an altar, and laid the wood in order upon it : and when he had bound Isaac his son, he laid him on the altar upon the pile of wood. And he put forth his hand and took the sword, to sacrifice his son. And behold an Angel of the Lord from heaven called to him, saying : Abraham, Abraham. And he answered : Here I am. And he said to him : Lay not thy hand upon the boy, neither do thou any thing to him : Now I know that thou fearest God, and hast not spared thy only begotten son for My sake. Abraham lifted up his eyes, and saw behind his back a ram amongst the briers sticking fast by the horns, which he took and offered for a holocaust instead of his son (*Gen.* xxii. 8).

Sacrifices, and oblations, and holocausts for sin, Thou wouldst not, neither are they pleasing to Thee, which are offered according to the law. Then said I, Behold, I come to do Thy will, O God : He taketh away the first, that He may establish that which followeth. In the which will, we are sanctified by the oblation of the body of Jesus Christ once (*Heb.* x. 8).

For if Thou hadst desired sacrifice, I would indeed have given it : with burnt-offerings Thou wilt not be delighted. A sacrifice to God is an afflicted spirit : a contrite and an humbled heart, O God, Thou wilt not despise. Deal favourably, O Lord, in Thy good-will with Sion ; that the walls of Jerusalem may be built up. Then shalt Thou accept the sacrifice of justice, oblations and whole burnt-offerings : then shall they lay calves upon Thy altar (*Ps.* l. 18).

For from the rising of the sun even to the going down, My name is great among the Gentiles, and in every place there is sacrifice, and there is offered to My Name a clean oblation : for My Name is great among the Gentiles, saith the Lord of Hosts (*Mal.* i. 11).

So also Christ was offered once to exhaust the sins of many : the second time He shall appear without sin, to them that expect Him unto salvation (*Heb.* ix. 28).

Q. Is it not also a memorial of the passion and death of our Lord ?

A. Yes ; for Christ, at His last supper, commanded it to be offered in remembrance of Him.

And He said to them : With desire I have desired to eat this pasch with you before I suffer. For I say to you, that from this time I will not eat it, till it be fulfilled in the kingdom of God. And having taken the chalice He gave thanks, and said : Take, and divide it among you. For I say to you, that I will not drink of the fruit of the vine, till the kingdom of God come (*S. Luke* xxii. 15).

For as often as you shall eat this bread, and drink the chalice, you shall shew the death of the Lord, until He come (1 *Cor.* xi. 26).

He hath made a remembrance of His wonderful works, being a merciful and gracious Lord : He hath given food to them that fear Him (*Ps.* cx. 4).

Q. How should we hear Mass ?

A. With great attention and devotion.

And the four living creatures had each of them six wings : and round about and within they are full of eyes. And they rested not day and night, saying, Holy, holy, holy, Lord God Almighty, who was, and who is, and who is to come. And when those living creatures gave glory and honour and benediction to Him that sitteth on the throne, who liveth for ever and ever : the four-and-twenty ancients fell down before Him that sitteth on the throne, and adored Him that liveth for ever and ever, and cast their crowns before the throne, saying : Thou art worthy, O Lord our God, to receive glory, and honour, and power : because Thou hast created all things, and for Thy will they were, and have been created (*Apoc.* iv. 8).

In the year that king Ozias died, I saw the Lord sitting upon a throne high and elevated : and His train filled the temple. Upon it stood the Seraphim : the one had six wings, and the other had six wings : with two they covered his face, and with two they covered his feet, and with two they flew. And they cried one to another, and said : Holy, holy, holy, the Lord God of Hosts, all the earth is full of His glory. And the lintels of the doors were moved at the voice of him that cried, and the house was filled with smoke. And I said : Woe is me, because I have held my peace ; because I am a man of unclean lips, and I dwell in the midst of a people that hath unclean lips, and I have seen with my eyes the King the Lord of Hosts. And one of the Seraphim flew to me, and in his hand was a live coal, which he had taken with the tongs off the altar. And he touched my mouth, and said : Behold this hath touched thy lips, and thy iniquities shall be taken away, and thy sin shall be cleansed (*Isa.* vi. 1).

When you come therefore together into one place, it is not now to eat the Lord's supper. For every one taketh before his own supper to eat. And one indeed is hungry, and another is drunk. What, have you not houses to eat and to drink in? Or despise ye the church of God : and put them to shame that have not? What shall I say to you? Do I praise you? In this I praise you not (1 *Cor.* xi. 20).

Who shall ascend into the mountain of the Lord : or who shall stand in His holy place? The innocent in hands, and clean of heart, who hath not taken his soul in vain, nor sworn deceitfully to his neighbour (*Ps.* xxiii. 3).

Lord, who shall dwell in Thy tabernacle? or who shall rest in Thy holy hill ? He that walketh without blemish and worketh justice : he that speaketh truth in his heart, who hath not used deceit in his tongue : nor hath done evil to his neighbour: nor taken up a reproach against his neighbours (*Ps.* xiv. 1).

For the sparrow hath found herself a house, and the turtle a nest for herself where she may lay her young ones : Thy altars, O Lord of Hosts, my King and my God. Blessed are they that dwell in Thy house, O Lord: they shall praise Thee for ever and ever (*Ps.* lxxxiii. 4).

And another Angel came, and stood before the altar, having a golden censer ; and there was given to him much incense, that he should offer of the prayers of all saints upon the golden altar, which is before the throne of God (*Apoc.* viii. 3).

Let my prayer be directed as incense in Thy sight : the lifting up of my hands, as evening sacrifice. Set a watch, O Lord, before my mouth : and a door round about my lips. Incline not my heart to evil words ; to make excuses in sins (*Ps.* cxl. 2).

Q. What is the sacrament of Penance ?

A. Penance is a sacrament whereby the sins which we have com-

In that day there shall be a fountain open to the house of David, and to the inhabitants of Jerusalem : for the washing of the sinner, and of the unclean woman (*Zach.* xiii. 1).

mitted after baptism are forgiven.

Thou shalt sprinkle me with hyssop, and I shall be cleansed : thou shalt wash me, and I shall be made whiter than snow (*Ps.* l. 5).

If your sins be as scarlet, they shall be made as white as snow : and if they be red as crimson, they shall be white as wool (*Isa.* i. 18).

Q. Does the sacrament of Penance forgive mortal sins only ?
A. No ; it forgives venial sins also ; and it likewise increases the grace of God in the soul.

For a just man shall fall seven times, and shall rise again : but the wicked shall fall down into evil (*Prov.* xxiv. 16).

And he that contemneth small things, shall fall by little and little (*Ecclus.* xix. 1).

Q. When did our Lord ordain this sacrament ?
A. When He breathed on His Apostles and said, "Whose sins you shall forgive, they are forgiven" (*S. John* xx. 23).

And I will give to thee the keys of the kingdom of heaven. And whatsoever thou shalt bind upon earth it shall be bound also in heaven : and whatsoever thou shalt loose on earth, it shall be loosed also in heaven (*S. Matt.* xvi. 19).

And when He had said this, He shewed them His hands, and His side. The disciples therefore were glad, when they saw the Lord. He said therefore to them again : Peace be to you. As the Father hath sent Me, I also send you. When He had said this, He breathed on them ; and He said to them : Receive ye the Holy Ghost. Whose sins you shall forgive, they are forgiven them ; and whose sins you shall retain, they are retained (*S. John* xx. 20).

Q. How is this forgiveness conveyed to our souls?
A. By the Priest's absolution, joined with contrition, confession, and satisfaction.

Now are you clean by reason of the word, which I have spoken to you (*S. John* xv. 33).

And behold they brought to Him one sick of the palsy lying in a bed. And Jesus, seeing their faith, said to the man sick of the palsy : Be of good heart, son, thy sins are forgiven thee. And behold some of

the scribes said within themselves :
He blasphemeth. And Jesus seeing their thoughts, said : Why do
you think evil in your hearts?
Whether it is easier to say, Thy sins
are forgiven thee : or to say, Arise
and walk ? But that you may know
that the Son of Man hath power on
earth to forgive sins (then said He
to the man sick of the palsy), Arise,
take up thy bed, and go into thy
house (*S. Matt.* ix. 2).

Q. What is the Priest's
absolution ?
A. It is the form of
words used by the
Priest: " I absolve thee
from thy sins, in the
Name of the Father, and
of the Son, and of the
Holy Ghost."

Amen I say to you, whatsoever
you shall bind upon earth, shall be
bound also in heaven : and whatsoever you shall loose upon earth,
shall be loosed also in heaven (*S.
Matt.* xviii. 18).

Q. What is contri-
tion ?
A. Contrition is a
hearty sorrow for our
sins, by which we have
offended so good a God,
with a firm purpose of
amendment.

A sacrifice to God is an afflicted
spirit: a contrite and humbled heart,
O God, thou wilt not despise (*Ps.*
l. 19).
The Lord buildeth up Jerusalem :
He will gather together the dispersed
of Israel. Who healeth the broken
of heart, and bindeth up their bruises
(*Ps.* cxlvi. 2).
Neither is there at this time
prince, or leader, or prophet, or
holocaust, or sacrifice, or oblation,
or incense, or place of first fruits
before Thee, that we may find Thy
mercy : nevertheless in a contrite
heart and humble spirit let us be
accepted (*Dan.* iii. 38).
I have laboured in my groanings,
every night I will wash my bed : I will
water my couch with my tears (*Ps.*
vi. 7).
The Lord is nigh unto them that
are of a contrite heart : and He will
save the humble of spirit (*Ps.* xxxiii.
9.

Q. What is a firm purpose of amendment?

A. It is a resolution, by the Grace of God, to avoid not only sin, but also the occasions of it.

Q. What is the best motive to be sorry for our sins?

A. The love of God, who is infinitely good in Himself, and infinitely good to us.

Q. What other motives have we to be sorry for our sins?

A. Because by them we lose Heaven, and deserve Hell.

Q. How may we obtain this hearty contrition for our sins?

A. We must earnestly beg it of God, and make use of such considerations as may move us to it.

But if the wicked do penance for all his sins, which he hath committed, and keep all My commandments, and do judgment, and justice, living he shall live, and shall not die. I will not remember all his iniquities that he hath done : in his justice which he hath wrought, he shall live. Is it My will that a sinner should die, saith the Lord God, and not that he should be converted from his ways and live? (*Ezech.* xviii. 21.)

And when the wicked turneth himself away from his wickedness, which he hath wrought, and doeth judgment, and justice: he shall save his soul alive. Because he considereth and turneth away himself from all his iniquities which he hath wrought, he shall surely live, and not die (*Ezech.* xviii. 27).

Say not : I have sinned, and what harm hath befallen me? for the Most High is a patient rewarder (*Ecclus.* v. 4).

And turning to the woman, He said unto Simon : Dost thou see this woman? I entered into thy house, thou gavest Me no water for My feet ; but she with tears hath washed My feet, and with her hairs hath wiped them. Thou gavest Me no kiss ; but she, since she came in, hath not ceased to kiss My feet. My head with oil thou didst not anoint; but she with ointment hath anointed My feet. Wherefore I say to thee : Many sins are forgiven her, because she hath loved much (*S. Luke* vii. 44).

We fools esteemed their life madness, and their end without honour. Behold how they are numbered among the children of God, and their lot is among the saints. Therefore we have erred from the way of truth, and the light of justice hath not shined unto us, and the sun of understanding hath not risen upon us. We wearied ourselves in the way of iniquity and destruction, and have walked through hard ways, but the way of the Lord we have not known (*Wisd.* v. 4).

Q. What is confession [1]?

A. It is to accuse ourselves of our sins to a Priest.

Q. What if one should wilfully conceal a mortal sin in confession?

A. He would commit a great sin by telling a lie to the Holy Ghost, and would make a bad confession.

If thou perceive that there be among you a hard and doubtful matter in judgment between blood and blood, cause and cause, leprosy and leprosy: and thou shalt see that the words of the judges within thy gates do vary: arise, and go up to the place, which the Lord thy God shall choose. And thou shalt come to the priests of the Levitical race, and to the judge, that shall be at that time: and thou shalt ask of them, and they shall shew thee the truth of the judgment (*Deut.* xvii. 8).

And He charged him that he should tell no man, but, Go, shew thyself to the priest, and offer for thy cleansing according as Moses commanded, for a testimony to them (*S. Luke* v. 14).

And many of them that believed, came confessing and declaring their deeds (*Acts* xix. 18).

Confess therefore your sins one to another: and pray one for another, that you may be saved (*S. James* v. 16).

I will recount to Thee all my years in the bitterness of my soul (*Isa.* xxxviii. 15).

Naaman was angry and went away, saying: I thought he would have come out to me, and standing would have invoked the Name of the Lord his God, and touched

---

[1] See note E, on Confession.

I

with his hand the place of the leprosy, and healed me. Are not the Abana, and the Pharphar, rivers of Damascus, better than all the waters of Israel, that I may wash in them, and be made clean? So as he turned, and was going away with indignation, his servants came to him, and said to him: Father, if the prophet had bid thee do some great thing, surely thou shouldst have done it: how much rather what he now hath said to thee: Wash, and thou shalt be clean? (4 *Kings* v. 11.)

Q. How many things have we to do in order to prepare for confession?
A. Four things. First. We must heartily pray to God for His grace to help us. Secondly.We must carefully examine our conscience. Thirdly We must beg pardon of God, and be very sorry from our hearts for having offended Him. And Fourthly. We must resolve to renounce our sins, and to begin a new life for the future.

Q. What is Satisfaction?
A. It is doing the penance given us by the Priest.

Say not: I have sinned, and what harm hath befallen me? for the Most High is a patient rewarder. Be not without fear about sin forgiven, and add not sin upon sin: and say not: The mercy of the Lord is great, He will have mercy on the multitude of thy sins. For mercy and wrath quickly come from Him, and His wrath looketh upon sinners. Delay not to be converted to the Lord, and defer it not from day to day. For His wrath shall come on a sudden, and in the time of vengeance He will destroy thee (*Ecclus* v. 4).

Now therefore saith the Lord: Be converted to Me with all your heart, in fasting, and in weeping, and in mourning. And rend your hearts, and not your garments, and turn to the Lord your God: for He is gracious and merciful, patient and rich in mercy, and ready to repent of the evil. Who knoweth but He will return, and forgive, and leave a blessing behind Him, sacrifice and libation to the Lord your God? (*Joel* ii. 12.)

They that fear the Lord, will prepare their hearts, and in His sight will sanctify their souls. They that fear the Lord, keep His commandments, and will have patience even until His visitation, saying: If we do not penance, we shall fall into the hands of the Lord, and not into the hands of men. For according to His greatness, so also is His mercy with Him (*Ecclus.* ii. 20).

Then began He to upbraid the cities wherein were done the most of His miracles, for that they had not done penance. Wo to thee, Corozain, wo to thee, Bethsaida: for if in Tyre and Sidon had been wrought the miracles that have been wrought in you, they had long ago done penance in sackcloth and ashes (*S. Matt.* xi. 20).

Q. What is an Indulgence?

A. An Indulgence is a remission of the temporal punishment which often remains due to sin, after its guilt has been forgiven.

Be not without fear about sin forgiven, and add not sin upon sin (*Ecclus.* v. 5).

And David said to Nathan: I have sinned against the Lord. And Nathan said to David: The Lord also hath taken away thy sin: thou shalt not die. Nevertheless, because thou hast given occasion to the enemies of the Lord to blaspheme, for this thing, the child that is born to thee, shall surely die (*2 Kings* xii. 13).

Q. What is Extreme Unction?

A. Extreme Unction is the anointing of the sick with holy oil, accompanied with prayer.

Q. When is this sacrament given?

A. When we are in danger of death by sickness.

And going forth they preached that men should do penance: and they cast out many devils, and anointed with oil many that were sick, and healed them (*S. Mark* vi. 12).

Q. What are the effects of this sacrament?

A. It comforts the soul in her last agony, it remits sin, and also restores health when God sees it expedient.

Q. What authority is there in Scripture for the sacrament of Extreme Unction?

A. In the 5th chapter of St. James it is said, " Is any man sick among you, let him bring in the Priests of the Church; and let them pray over him, anointing him with oil, in the Name of the Lord; and the prayer of faith shall save the sick man; and the Lord shall raise him up: and if he be in sins, they shall be forgiven him " (*S. James* v. 14, 15).

Q. What is Holy Order?

A. Holy Order is a sacrament by which Bishops, Priests, and other Ministers of the Church are ordained, and receive power and grace to perform their sacred duties.

He said therefore to them again: Peace be to you. As the Father hath sent Me, I also send you (*S. John* xx. 21).

And Jesus coming, spoke to them, saying: All power is given to me in heaven and in earth. Going therefore, teach ye all nations; baptizing them in the Name of the Father, and of the Son, and of the Holy Ghost, teaching them to observe all things whatsoever I have commanded you: and behold I am with you all days, even to the consummation of the world (*S. Matt.* xxviii. 18).

And taking bread, He gave thanks, and brake: and gave to them, saying: This is My body which is

given for you. Do this for a commemoration of Me (*S. Luke* xxii.
19).

When He had said this, He
breathed on them; and He said to
them: Receive ye the Holy Ghost.
Whose sins you shall forgive, they
are forgiven them: and whose sins
you shall retain, they are retained
(*S. John* xx. 22).

These they set before the apostles:
and they praying imposed hands
upon them (*Acts* vi. 6).

And as they were ministering to
the Lord, and fasting, the Holy
Ghost said to them: Separate me
Saul and Barnabas, for the work
whereunto I have taken them. Then
they fasting and praying, and imposing their hands upon them, sent
them away (*Acts* xiii. 2).

And when they had ordained to
them priests in every church, and
had prayed with fasting, they com-
mended them to the Lord, in whom
they believed (*Acts* xiv. 22).

And the things, which thou hast
heard of me by many witnesses, the
same commend to faithful men, who
shall be fit to teach others also (2
Tim. ii. 2).

Let no man despise thy youth:
but be thou an example of the faithful, in word, in conversation, in charity, in faith, in chastity. Till I
come, attend unto reading, to exhortation, and to doctrine. Neglect
not the grace that is in thee, which
was given thee by prophecy, with
imposition of the hands of the priesthood (1 *Tim.* iv. 12).

Obey your prelates, and be subject
to them. For they watch as being
to render an account of your souls;
that they may do this with joy, and
not with grief. For this is not expedient for you (*Heb.* xiii. 17).

Let a man so account of us as of the ministers of Christ, and the dispensers of the mysteries of God. Here now it is required among the dispensers, that a man be found faithful. But to me it is a very small thing to be judged by you, or by man's day : but neither do I judge my own self. For I am not conscious to myself of any thing, yet am I not hereby justified : but he that judgeth me, is the Lord (1 *Cor.* iv. 1).

For which cause I admonish thee, that thou stir up the grace of God which is in thee by the imposition of my hands (2 *Tim.* i. 6).

Upon thy walls, O Jerusalem, I have appointed watchmen all the day, and all the night, they shall never hold their peace (*Isa.* lxii. 6).

For the lips of the priest shall keep knowledge, and they shall seek the law at his mouth : because he is the Angel of the Lord of hosts (*Mal.* ii. 7).

The Lord is the portion of my inheritance and of my cup : it is Thou that wilt restore my inheritance to me (*Ps.* xv. 5).

Q. What is Matrimony?

A. Matrimony is a sacrament by which the contract of marriage is blessed and sanctified.

Q. What grace does this sacrament give to those who receive it worthily?

A. It enables them to bear the difficulties of their state, to love and be faithful to one another, and to bring

Let women be subject to their husbands, as to the Lord. Because the husband is the head of the wife : as Christ is the head of the church. He is the saviour of His body. Therefore as the church is subject to Christ, so also let the wives be to their husbands in all things. Husbands, love your wives, as Christ also loved the church, and delivered Himself up for it : that He might sanctify it cleansing it by the laver of water in the word of life. That He might present it to Himself a glorious church, not having spot or wrinkle, or any such thing, but that it should up their children in the fear of God.

be holy and without blemish. So also ought men to love their wives as their own bodies. He that loveth his wife loveth himself. For no man ever hateth his own flesh : but nourisheth and cherisheth it, as also Christ doth the church: because we are members of His body, of His flesh, and of His] bones. For this cause shall a man leave his father and mother : and shall cleave to his wife, and they shall be two in one flesh. This is a great sacrament ; but I speak in Christ and in the church. Nevertheless let every one of you in particular love his wife as himself; and let the wife fear her husband (*Eph.* v. 22).

Let the husband render the debt to his wife : and the wife also in like manner to the husband. The wife hath not the power of her own body ; but the husband. And in like manner the husband also hath not power of his own body ; but the wife. Defraud not one another, except, perhaps by consent, for a time, that you may give yourselves to prayer : and return together again, lest Satan tempt you for your incontinency. But I speak this by indulgence, not by commandment (1 *Cor.* vii. 3).

Happy is the husband of a good wife : for the number of his years is double. A virtuous woman rejoiceth her husband, and shall fulfil the years of his life in peace. A good wife is a good portion, she shall be given in a portion of them that fear God, to a man for his good deeds (*Ecclus.* xxvi. 1).

Every man that passeth beyond his own bed, despising his own soul, and saying : Who seeth me ? darkness compasseth me about, and the walls cover me, and no man seeth me : whom do I fear ? the Most High will not remember my sins. And he understandeth not that His eye seeth all things, for such a man's fear driveth from him the fear of God, and the eyes of men fearing him : and he knoweth not that the eyes of the Lord are far brighter than the sun, beholding round about all the ways of men, and the bottom of the deep, and looking into the hearts of men into the most hidden parts. For all things were known to the Lord God, before they were created : so also after they were perfected He beholdeth all things (*Ecclus.* xxiii. 25).

Q. Can any human power dissolve the bond of marriage?
A. No; for Christ has said, "What God hath joined together, let no man put asunder" (*Matt.* xix. 6).

And I say to you, that whosoever shall put away his wife, except it be for fornication, and shall marry another, committeth adultery : and he that shall marry her that is put away, committeth adultery (*S. Matt.* xix. 9).

CHAPTER VII.

OF VIRTUE AND VICES.

Q. How many Theological Virtues are there?
A. Three: Faith, Hope, and Charity.

Q. Why are they called Theological?
A. Because they relate immediately to God.

And now there remain, faith, hope, charity, these three : but the greater of these is charity (1 *Cor.* xiii. 13).
Now faith is the substance of things to be hoped for, the evidence of things that appear not. For by this the ancients obtained a testimony. By faith we understand that the world was framed by the word

Q. What does Faith enable us to do?

A. It enables us to believe without doubting all that God has taught and the Church proposes.

of God; that from invisible things visible things might be made (*Heb.* xi. 1).

But without faith it is impossible to please God. For he that cometh to God, must believe that He is, and is a rewarder to them that seek Him (*Heb.* xi. 6).

And we have the more firm prophetical word : whereunto you do well to attend, as to a light that shineth in a dark place, until the day dawn, and the day-star arise in your hearts. Understanding this first, that no prophecy of scripture is made by private interpretation (2 *Pet.* i. 19).

Q. What does Hope enable us to do?

A. It enables us to expect with confidence that God will give us salvation, and all things necessary to obtain it, if we do what He requires of us.

And not only so; but we glory also in tribulations, knowing that tribulation worketh patience, and patience trial; and trial hope, and hope confoundeth not (*Rom.* v. 3).

In Thee, O Lord, have I hoped, let me never be confounded: deliver me in Thy justice (*Ps.* xxx. 2).

They that trust in the Lord shall be as mount Sion : he shall not be moved for ever that dwelleth in Jerusalem (*Ps.* cxxiv. 1).

For I know whom I have believed, and I am certain that He is able to keep that which I have committed unto Him, against that day (2 *Tim.* i. 12).

Why art thou sad, O my soul? and why dost thou trouble me? Hope in God, for I will still give praise to Him: the salvation of my countenance, and my God (*Ps.* xli. 6).

Many are the scourges of the sinner, but mercy shall encompass him that hopeth in the Lord (*Ps.* xxxi. 10).

Q. What does Charity enable us to do?

Let us therefore love God, because God first hath loved us. If

A. It enables us to love God above all things, and our neighbours as ourselves.

any man say, I love God, and hateth his brother : he is a liar. For he that loveth not his brother, whom he seeth, how can he love God, whom he seeth not? And this commandment we have from God, that he, who loveth God, love also his brother (1 *S. John* iv. 19).

For I am sure that neither death, nor life, nor Angels, nor principalities, nor powers, nor things present, nor things to come, nor might, nor height, nor depth, nor any other creature shall be able to separate us from the love of God, which is in Christ Jesus our Lord (*Rom.* viii. 38).

If any man love not our Lord Jesus Christ, let him be anathema, Maran Atha (1 *Cor.* xvi. 22).

As the Father hath loved Me, I also have loved you. Abide in My love. If you keep My commandments, you shall abide in My love (*S. John* xv. 9).

And if I should distribute all my goods to feed the poor, and if I should deliver my body to be burned, and have not charity, it profiteth me nothing. Charity is patient, is kind : charity envieth not, dealeth not perversely, is not puffed up, is not ambitious, seeketh not her own, is not provoked to anger, thinketh no evil, rejoiceth not in iniquity, but rejoiceth with the truth : beareth all things, believeth all things, hopeth all things, endureth all things. Charity never falleth away: whether prophecies shall be made void, or tongues shall cease, or knowledge shall be destroyed (1 *Cor.* xiii. 3).

Owe no man any thing, but to love one another. For he that loveth his neighbour, hath fulfilled the law. For thou shalt not commit adultery, thou shalt not kill, thou shalt not steal, thou shalt not bear false witness, thou shalt not covet: and if there be any other commandment, it is comprised in this word, Thou shalt love thy neighbour as thyself. The love of our neighbour worketh no evil. Love therefore is the fulfilling of the law (*Rom.* xiii. 8).

Q. How many are the Cardinal Virtues?

A. Four: Prudence, Justice, Fortitude, and Temperance.

For the wisdom of the flesh is death: but the wisdom of the Spirit is life and peace. Because the wisdom of the flesh is an enemy to God: for it is not subject to the law of God, neither can it be (*Rom.* viii. 6).

For I say, through the grace that is given me, to all that are among you, not to be more wise than it behoveth to be wise, but to be wise unto sobriety (*Rom.* xii. 3).

The justice of the upright shall make his way prosperous: and the wicked man shall fall by his own wickedness. The justice of the righteous shall deliver them: and the unjust shall be caught in their own snares (*Prov.* xi. 5).

Behold I send you as sheep in the midst of wolves. Be ye therefore wise as serpents and simple as doves (*S. Matt.* x. 16).

And be not drunk with wine, wherein is luxury, but be ye filled with the Holy Spirit (*Eph.* v. 18).

Q. What are the two precepts of Charity?

A. 1. Thou shalt love the Lord thy God with thy whole heart, with thy whole soul, with all thy strength, and with all thy mind. 2. And thy neighbour as thyself.

And one of them, a doctor of the law, asked Him, tempting Him: Master, which is the great commandment in the law? Jesus said to him: Thou shalt love the Lord thy God with thy whole heart, and with thy whole soul, and with thy whole mind. This is the greatest and the first commandment. And the second is like to this: Thou shalt love thy neighbour as thyself. On these two commandments dependeth the whole law and the prophets (*S. Matt.* xxii. 35).

Q. Say the seven Corporal Works of Mercy.

A. 1. To feed the hungry. 2. To give drink to the thirsty. 3. To clothe the naked. 4. To harbour the harbourless. 5. To visit the sick. 6. To visit the imprisoned. 7. To bury the dead.

Then shall the King say to them that shall be on His right hand : Come, ye blessed of My Father, possess you the kingdom prepared for you from the foundation of the world. For I was hungry, and you gave Me to eat : I was thirsty, and you gave Me to drink : I was a stranger, and you took Me in : naked, and you covered Me : sick, and you visited Me : I was in prison, and you came to Me. Then shall the just answer Him, saying : Lord, when did we see Thee hungry, and fed Thee; thirsty, and gave Thee drink ? and when did we see Thee a stranger, and took Thee in ? or naked, and covered Thee ? or when did we see Thee sick or in prison, and came to Thee ? and the King answering, shall say to them : Amen I say to you, as long as you did it to one of these My least brethren, you did it to Me (*S. Matt.* xxv. 34).

And whosoever shall give to drink to one of those little ones a cup of cold water only in the name of a disciple, amen I say to you, he shall not lose his reward (*S. Matt.* x. 42).

And if a brother or sister be naked, and want daily food : and one of you say to them : Go in peace, be you warmed and filled : yet give them not those things that are necessary for the body : what shall it profit ? (*S. James* ii. 15).

He that hath the substance of this world, and shall see his brother in need, and shall shut up his bowels from him : how doth the charity of God abide in him ? My little children, let us not love in word, nor in tongue, but in deed, and in truth (1 *S. John* iii. 17).

When thou didst pray with tears, and didst bury the dead, and didst leave thy dinner, and hide the dead by day in thy house, and bury them by night, I offered thy prayer to the Lord (*Tobias* xii. 12).

Q. Say the seven Spiritual Works of Mercy.

A. 1. To convert the sinner. 2. To instruct the ignorant. 3. To counsel the doubtful. 4. To comfort the sorrowful. 5. To bear wrongs patiently. 6. To forgive injuries. 7. To pray for the living and the dead.

But they that are learned shall shine as the brightness of the firmament : and they that instruct many to justice, as stars for all eternity (*Dan.* xii. 3).

Brethren, and if a man be overtaken in any fault, you, who are spiritual, instruct such a one in the spirit of meekness, considering thyself, lest thou also be tempted. Bear ye one another's burdens : and so you shall fulfil the law of Christ (*Gal.* vi. 1).

But if thy brother shall offend against thee, go, and rebuke him between thee and him alone. If he shall hear thee, thou shalt gain thy brother. But if he will not hear thee, take with thee one or two more : that in the mouth of two or three witnesses every word may stand (*S. Matt.* xviii. 15).

Q. Say the eight Beatitudes.

A. 1. Blessed are the poor in spirit ; for theirs is the kingdom of heaven.

2. Blessed are the meek ; for they shall possess the land.

3. Blessed are they that mourn ; for they shall be comforted.

4. Blessed are they that hunger and thirst after justice ; for they shall have their fill.

5. Blessed are the

Then Jesus said to his disciples : Amen I say to you, that a rich man shall hardly enter into the kingdom of heaven. And again I say to you : It is easier for a camel to pass through the eye of a needle, than for a rich man to enter into the kingdom of heaven (*S. Matt.* xix. 23).

He hath filled the hungry with good things : and the rich he hath sent empty away (*S. Luke* i. 53).

merciful ; for they shall obtain mercy.

6. Blessed are the clean of heart ; for they shall see God.

7. Blessed are the peace-makers ; for they shall be called the children of God.

8. Blessed are they that suffer persecution for justice-sake ; for theirs is the kingdom of heaven.

Q. Say the seven deadly sins.

A. Pride, Covetousness, Lust, Anger, Gluttony, Envy, Sloth.— Contrary virtues :—Humility, Liberality, Chastity, Meekness, Temperance, Brotherly love, Diligence.

Behold this was the iniquity of Sodom thy sister, pride, fulness of bread, and abundance, and the idleness of her, and of her daughters : and they did not put forth their hand to the needy, and to the poor (*Ezech.* xvi. 49).

For all that is in the world is the concupiscence of the flesh, and the concupiscence of the eyes, and the pride of life, which is not of the Father, but is of the world. And the world passeth away, and the concupiscence thereof. But he that doth the will of God, abideth for ever (1 *S. John* ii. 16).

In like manner, ye young men, be subject to the ancients. And do you all insinuate humility one to another, for God resisteth the proud, but to the humble He giveth grace. Be you humbled therefore under the mighty hand of God, that He may exalt you in the time of visitation (1 *S. Pet.* v. 5).

And He said : Amen I say to you, unless you be converted, and become as little children, you shall not enter into the kingdom of heaven. Whosoever therefore shall humble himself as this little child, he is the greater in the kingdom of heaven (*S. Matt.* xviii. 3).

For know ye this and understand that no fornicator, nor unclean, nor covetous person (which is a serving of idols,) hath inheritance in the kingdom of Christ and of God (*Eph.* v. 5).

For to him that is little, mercy is granted : but the mighty shall be mightily tormented. For God will not except any man's person, neither will He stand in awe of any man's greatness : for He made the little and the great, and He hath equally care of all. But a greater punishment is ready for the more mighty (*Wisd.* vi. 7).

Q. Say the sins against the Holy Ghost.

A. 1. Presumption of God's mercy. 2. Despair. 3. Resisting the known truth. 4. Envy at another's spiritual good. 5. Obstinacy in sin. 6. Final impenitence.

But he that shall blaspheme against the Holy Ghost, shall never have forgiveness, but shall be guilty of an everlasting sin (*S. Mark* iii. 29).

And Peter answering, said to him : Although all shall be scandalized in Thee, I will never be scandalized. Jesus said to him : Amen I say to thee, that in this night before the cock crow, thou wilt deny me thrice (*S. Matt.* xxvi. 33).

Then Judas, who betrayed Him, seeing that He was condemned, repenting himself, brought back the thirty pieces of silver to the chief-priests and ancients. Saying : I have sinned in betraying innocent blood. But they said : What is that to us ? look thou to it. And casting down the pieces of silver in the temple, he departed : and went and hanged himself with a halter (*S. Matt.* xxvii. 3).

You stiff-necked and uncircumcized in heart and ears, you always resist the Holy Ghost : as your fathers did, so do you also. Which of the prophets have not your fathers persecuted ? and they have slain them who foretold · of the coming of the Just One; of whom you have been now the betrayers and murderers (*Acts* vii. 51).

And the Lord had respect to Abel, and to his offerings. But to Cain and his offerings he had no respect : and Cain was exceedingly angry, and his countenance fell. And the Lord said to him : Why art thou angry? and why is thy countenance fallen? if thou do well, shalt thou not receive? but if ill, shall not sin forthwith be present at the door? but the lust thereof shall be under thee, and thou shalt have dominion over it (*Gen.* iv. 4).

And Pharao's heart was hardened, neither did he hear them, as the Lord had commanded. And he turned himself away, and went into his house; neither did he set his heart to it this time also (*Exod.* vii. 22).

Or despisest thou the riches of his goodness, and patience, and long-suffering? knowest thou not that the benignity of God leadeth thee to penance? but according to thy hardness and impenitent heart, thou treasurest up to thyself wrath, against the day of wrath and revelation of the just judgment of God (*Rom.* ii. 4).

Q. Say the four sins crying to Heaven for vengeance.

A. 1. Wilful murder. 2. Sodomy. 3. Oppression of the poor. 4. Defrauding labourers of their wages.

And the Lord said to Cain : Where is thy brother Abel? and he answered, I know not : am I my brother's keeper? and He said to him : What hast thou done? the voice of thy brother's blood crieth to Me from the earth. Now, therefore, cursed shalt thou be upon the earth, which hath opened her mouth and received the blood of thy brother at thy hand (*Gen.* iv. 9).

And the Lord said : The cry of Sodom and Gomorrha is multiplied, and their sin is become exceedingly grievous (*Gen.* xviii. 20).

As Sodom and Gomorrha, and the neighbouring cities, in like manner, having given themselves over to fornication, and going after other flesh, were made an example, suffering the punishment of eternal fire. In like manner these men also defile the flesh, and despise dominion, and blaspheme majesty (*S. Jude* 7).

Behold the hire of the labourers, who have reaped down your fields, which by fraud have been kept back by you, crieth : and the cry of them hath entered into the ears of the Lord of Sabaoth (*S. James* v. 4).

Wo to him that buildeth up his house by injustice, and his chambers not in judgment : that will oppress his friend without cause, and will not pay him his wages (*Jer.* xxii. 13).

Q. Are we ever answerable for the sins of others?

A. Yes ; as often as we are the cause of their sins through our own fault.

Who can understand sins ? from my secret ones cleanse me, O Lord : and from those of others spare thy servant (*Ps.* xviii. 13).

Q. In how many ways may this happen?

A. In nine ways :—
1. By counsel. 2. By command. 3. By consent. 4. By provocation. 5. By praise or flattery. 6. By concealment. 7. By partaking. 8. By silence. 9. By defence of the ill done.

Q. Say the three Eminent Good Works.

A. Prayer, Fasting, and Almsdeeds.

Prayer is good with fasting and alms, more than to lay up treasures of gold : for alms delivereth from death, and the same is that which

K

purgeth away sins, and maketh to find mercy and life everlasting (*Tobias* xii. 8).

And in that day you shall not ask Me any thing. Amen, amen I say to you : if you ask the Father any thing in My Name, He will give it you (*S. John* xvi. 23).

And whosoever shall give to drink to one of those little ones a cup of cold water only in the name of a disciple, amen I say to you, he shall not lose his reward (*S. Matt.* x. 42).

And He said to him : Thy prayers and thy alms are ascended for a memorial in the sight of God (*Acts* x. 4).

Deal thy bread to the hungry, and bring the needy and the harbourless into thy house : when thou shalt see one naked, cover him, and despise not thy own flesh. Then shall thy light break forth as the morning, and thy health shall speedily arise, and thy justice shall go before thy face, and the glory of the Lord shall gather thee up (*Isa.* lviii. 7).

Poverty.

Q. Say the Evangelical Counsels.

A. Voluntary Poverty, perpetual Chastity, and entire Obedience.

Jesus saith to him : If thou wilt be perfect, go, sell what thou hast, and give to the poor, and thou shalt have treasure in heaven : and come, follow Me. And when the young man had heard this word, he went away sad : for he had great possessions. Then Jesus said to His disciples : Amen I say to you, that a rich man shall hardly enter into the kingdom of heaven (*S. Matt.* xix. 21).

Hearken, my dearest brethren : hath not God chosen the poor in this world, rich in faith, and heirs of the kingdom which God hath promised to them that love Him ? (*S. James* ii. 5.)

Chastity.

His disciples say unto Him: If the case of a man with his wife be so, it is not expedient to marry. Who said to them: All men take not this word, but they to whom it is given. For there are eunuchs, who were born so from their mother's womb: and there are eunuchs, who were made so by men: and there are eunuchs who have made themselves eunuchs for the kingdom of heaven. He that can take, let him take it (*S. Matt.* xix. 10).

But I would have you to be without solicitude. He that is without a wife, is solicitous for the things that belong to the Lord how he may please God. But he that is with a wife, is solicitous for the things of the world, how he may please his wife; and he is divided. And the unmarried woman and the virgin thinketh on the things of the Lord : that she may be holy both in body and in spirit. But she that is married thinketh on the things of the world, how she may please her husband (1 *Cor.* vii. 32).

But if any man think that he seemeth dishonoured with regard to his virgin, for that she is above the age, and it must be so: let him do what he will: he sinneth not, if she marry. For he that hath determined being steadfast in his heart, having no necessity, but having power of his own will, and hath judged this in his heart, to keep his virgin, doth well. Therefore both he that giveth his virgin in marriage, doth well: and he that giveth her not, doth better (1 *Cor.* vii. 36).

And I beheld: and lo a Lamb stood upon Mount Sion, and with him an hundred forty-four thousand

K 2

having His Name, and the Name of His Father written on their foreheads. And I heard a voice from heaven, as the voice of many waters, and as the voice of great thunder : and the voice, which I heard, was as the voice of harpers, harping on their harps. And they sung as it were a new canticle, before the throne, and before the four living creatures, and the ancients : and no man could say the canticle, but those hundred forty-four thousand, who were purchased from the earth. These are they who were not defiled with women : for they are virgins. These follow the Lamb whithersoever he goeth. These were purchased from among men, the first-fruits to God and to the Lamb (*Apoc.* xiv. 1).

Obedience.

Be ye subject therefore to every human creature for God's sake (1 *Pet.* ii. 13).

And Samuel said : Doth the Lord desire holocausts and victims, and not rather that the voice of the Lord should be obeyed ? For obedience is better than sacrifices : and to hearken rather than to offer the fat of rams. Because it is like the sin of witchcraft, to rebel : and like the crime of idolatry, to refuse to obey. Forasmuch therefore as thou hast rejected the word of the Lord, the Lord hath also rejected thee from being king (1 *Kings* xv. 22).

Q. Say the four last things to be remembered.

A. Death, Judgment, Hell, Heaven.

It is appointed unto men once to die, and, after this, the judgment (*Heb.* ix. 27).

But the end of all is at hand. Be prudent therefore, and watch in prayers (1 *Pet.* iv. 7).

In all thy works remember thy

last end, and thou shalt never sin (*Ecclus.* vii. 40).

Amen, amen I say to you, unless the grain of wheat falling into the ground, die, itself remaineth alone. But if it die, it bringeth forth much fruit. He that loveth his life shall lose it : and he that hateth his life in this world keepeth it unto life eternal (*S. John* xii. 24).

For to me, to live is Christ : and to die is gain. And if to live in the flesh, this is to me the fruit of labour, and what I shall choose I know not. But I am straitened between two ; having a desire to be dissolved and to be with Christ, a thing by far the better (*Phil.* i. 21).

I beheld till thrones were placed, and the Ancient of days sat : His garment was white as snow, and the hair of His head like clean wool : His throne like flames of fire : the wheels of it like a burning fire. A swift stream of fire issued forth from before Him : thousands of thousands ministered to Him, and ten thousand times a hundred thousand stood before Him : the judgment sat and the books were opened (*Dan.* vii. 9).

And I saw the dead, great and small, standing in the presence of the throne, and the books were opened : and another book was opened, which is the book of life : and the dead were judged by those things which were written in the books, according to their works (*Apoc.* xx. 12).

Blessed are they that wash their robes in the blood of the Lamb : that they may have a right to the tree of life, and may enter in by the gates into the city. Without are dogs, and sorcerers, and unchaste, and murderers, and servers of idols, and every one that loveth and maketh a lie (*Apoc.* xxii. 14).

---•---

CHAPTER VIII.

THE CHRISTIAN'S RULE OF LIFE.

Q. What rule of life must we follow, if we hope to be saved?

A. We must follow the rule of life taught by Jesus Christ.

Jesus saith to him : I am the way, and the truth, and the life. No man cometh to the Father, but by Me (*S. John* xiv. 6).

I am the door. By Me, if any man enter in, he shall be saved: and he shall go in, and go out, and shall find pastures (*S. John* x. 9).

That was the true light, which enlighteneth every man that cometh into this world (*S. John* i. 9).

Q. What are we bound to do by this rule?

A. We are bound always to hate sin and to love God.

I have hated and abhorred iniquity; but I have loved thy law (*Ps.* cxviii. 163).

Thou hast loved justice, and hated iniquity : therefore God, thy God hath anointed thee with the oil of gladness above thy fellows (*Ps.* xliv. 8).

Hating that which is evil, cleaving to that which is good (*Rom.* xii. 9).

Q. How must we hate sin?

A. Above all other evils ; so as to be resolved never to commit a wilful sin for the love or fear of any thing whatsoever.

Flee from sins as from the face of a serpent : for if thou comest near them, they will take hold of thee. The teeth thereof are the teeth of a lion, killing the souls of men. All iniquity is like a two-edged sword, there is no remedy for the wound thereof (*Ecclus.* xxi. 2).

For I am sure that neither death, nor life, nor Angels, nor principalities, nor powers, nor things present, nor things to come, nor might, nor height, nor depth, nor any other creature shall be able to separate us from the love of God, which is in Christ Jesus our Lord (*Rom.* viii. 38).

And if thy right eye scandalize thee, pluck it out and cast it from thee. For it is expedient for thee that one of thy members should perish, rather than thy whole body be cast into hell. And if thy right hand scandalize thee, cut it off, and cast it from thee; for it is expedient for thee that one of thy members should perish, rather than that thy whole body go into hell (*S. Matt.* v. 29).

Q. How must we love God?

A. Above all things, and with our whole heart.

Q. How must we learn to love God?

A. We must beg of God to teach us. "O my God, teach me to love Thee!"

Q. What else must we do?

A. We must often think how good God is; often speak to Him in our hearts; and always seek to please Him.

And Jesus answered him: The first commandment of all is, Hear, O Israel: the Lord thy God is one God. And thou shalt love the Lord thy God with thy whole heart, and with thy whole soul, and with thy whole mind, and with thy whole strength. This is the first commandment. And the second is like to it: Thou shalt love thy neighbour as thyself. There is no other commandment greater than these. And the scribe said to Him: Well, Master, Thou hast said in truth, that there is one God, and there is no other besides Him. And that He should be loved with the whole heart, and with the whole understanding, and with the whole soul, and with the whole strength: and to love one's neighbour as oneself, is a greater thing than all holocausts and sacrifices (*S. Mark* xii. 29).

Q. And does not Jesus Christ teach us also to love one another?

A. Yes; He commands

But I say to you, Love your enemies: do good to them that hate you: and pray for them that persecute and calumniate you: that you us to love all persons without exception for His sake.

Q. How are we to love one another?

A. By wishing well to all, and praying for all; and never allowing ourselves any thought, word, or deed, to the injury of any one.

Q. And are we also to love our enemies?

A. Yes, we are; not only by forgiving them from our hearts, but also by wishing them well, and praying for them.

Q. What other rules does Jesus Christ give us?

A. To deny ourselves, to take up our Cross and to follow Him (*Matt.* xvi. 24).

Q. How are we to deny ourselves?

A. By giving up our own will, and by going against our own humours, inclinations, and passions.

Q. Why are we bound to deny ourselves in this manner?

A. Because our natural inclinations are prone to evil from our very childhood; and if not

may be the children of your Father who is in heaven, who maketh His sun to rise upon the good and bad, and raineth upon the just and the unjust (*S. Matt.* v. 44).

For all the law is fulfilled in one word: Thou shalt love thy neighbour as thyself (*Gal.* v. 14).

For if you love them that love you, what reward shall you have? Do not even the publicans this? And if you salute your brethren only, what do you more? do not also the heathens this? (*S. Matt.* v. 46.)

Enter ye in at the narrow gate: for wide is the gate, and broad is the way that leadeth to destruction, and many there are who go in thereat. How narrow is the gate, and strait is the way that leadeth to life: and few there are that find it! (*S. Matt.* vii. 13.)

Therefore, brethren, we are debtors, not to the flesh, to live according to the flesh. For if you live according to the flesh, you shall die. But if by the spirit you mortify the deeds of the flesh, you shall live. For whosoever are led by the Spirit of God, they are the sons of God (*Rom.* viii. 12).

For the flesh lusteth against the spirit: and the spirit against the flesh; for these are contrary one to another: so that you do not the things that you would (*Gal.* v. 17).

corrected by self-denial, they will certainly carry us to hell.

Q. How are we to take up our cross?

A. By submitting with patience to the labours and sufferings of this short life, and embracing them willingly for the love of God.

And whosoever doth not carry his cross and come after Me, cannot be My disciple (*S. Luke* xiv. 27).

Q. How are we to follow Christ?

A. By walking in His footsteps and imitating His virtues.

The disciple is not above his Master: but every one shall be perfect, if he be as his Master (*S. Luke* vi. 40).

Wherefore I beseech you, be ye followers of me, as I also am of Christ (1 *Cor.* iv. 16).

Q. What are the principal virtues we are to learn of Him?

A. Meekness, Humility, and Obedience.

Come to Me, all you that labour, and are burdened, and I will refresh you. Take up My yoke upon you, and learn of Me, because I am meek, and humble of heart: and you shall find rest to your souls. For My yoke is sweet and My burden light (*S. Matt.* xi. 28).

In your patience you shall possess your souls (*S. Luke* xxi. 19).

But I say to you not to resist evil : but if one strike thee on thy right cheek, turn to him the other also (*S. Matt.* v. 39).

Holocausts for sin did not please Thee. Then said I : Behold I come : in the head of the book it is written of me : that I should do Thy will, O God (*Heb.* x. 6).

Q. Which are the enemies the Christian must fight against all the days of his life?

A. The devil, the world, and the flesh.

Put you on the armour of God, that you may be able to stand against the deceits of the devil (*Eph.* vi. 11).

Love not the world, nor the things which are in the world. If any man love the world, the charity of the Father is not in him (1 *S. John* ii. 15).

Q. What do you mean by the devil?

A. Satan and all his wicked angels, who are ever seeking to draw us into sin, that we may be damned with them.

Be sober and watch : because your adversary the devil, as a roaring lion, goeth about seeking whom he may devour. Whom resist ye, strong in faith (1 *Pet.* v. 8).

And the seventy-two returned with joy, saying: Lord, the devils also are subject to us in Thy name. And He said to them : I saw Satan like lightning falling from heaven (*S. Luke* x. 17).

And lest the greatness of the revelations should lift me up, there was given me a sting of my flesh, an angel of Satan to buffet me (2 *Cor.* xii. 7).

And no wonder: for Satan himself transformeth himself into an Angel of light (2 *Cor.* xi. 14).

Q. What do you mean by the world?

A. All wicked company, and all such as love the vanities, riches, and pleasures of this world better than God.

If the world hate you, know ye that it hated Me before you. If you had been of the world : the world would love its own: but because you are not of the world, but I have chosen you out of the world, therefore the world hateth you (*S. John* xv. 18).

Adulterers, know you not that the friendship of this world, is the enemy of God? Whosoever therefore will be a friend of this world, becometh an enemy of God (*S. James* iv. 4).

Q. Why do you number these amongst the enemies of the soul?

A. Because they are always seeking, by word or example, to carry us along with them in the broad road that leads to damnation.

But wo to you that are rich : for you have your consolation. Wo to you that are filled: for you shall hunger. Wo to you that now laugh : for you shall mourn and weep (*S. Luke* vi. 24).

They have slept their sleep : and all the men of riches have found nothing in their hands (*Ps.* lxxv. 6).

Enter ye in at the narrow gate :

for wide is the gate, and broad is the way that leadeth to destruction, and many there are who go in thereat. How narrow is the gate, and strait is the way that leadeth to life : and few there are that find it ! (*S. Matt.* vii. 13.)

The congregation of sinners is like tow heaped together, and the end of them is a flame of fire. The way of sinners is made plain with stones, and in their end is hell, and darkness, and pains (*Ecclus.* xxi. 10).

Q. What do you mean by the flesh ?
A. Our own corrupt inclinations and passions, which are the most dangerous of all our enemies.

I say then, walk in the spirit, and you shall not fulfil the lusts of the flesh. For the flesh lusteth against the spirit : and the spirit against the flesh ; for these are contrary one to another : so that you do not the things that you would (*Gal.* v. 16).

But I see another law in my members, fighting against the law of my mind, and captivating me in the law of sin, that is in my members. Unhappy man that I am, who shall deliver me from the body of this death ? (*Rom.* vii. 23.)

Q. What must we do to hinder these enemies from drawing us into sin?
A. We must watch, pray, and fight against all their suggestions and temptations.

Watch ye, and pray that ye enter not into temptation. The spirit indeed is willing but the flesh weak (*S. Matt.* xxvi. 41).

Be subject therefore to God, but resist the devil, and he will fly from you. Draw nigh to God, and He will draw nigh to you. Cleanse your hands, ye sinners : and purify your hearts, ye double minded (*S. James* iv. 7).

Q. Whom must we depend upon in this warfare ?
A. Not upon ourselves, but upon God alone.

Unless the Lord build the house, they labour in vain that build it. Unless the Lord keep the city, he watcheth in vain that keepeth it (*Ps.* cxxvi. 1).

CHAPTER IX.

THE CHRISTIAN'S DAILY EXERCISE.

Q. What is the first thing you should do in the morning?

A. I should make the sign of the cross, and say, O my God, I offer my heart and soul to Thee.

Q. What should you do next?

A. I should rise diligently,. dress myself modestly, and occupy myself with good thoughts.

Q. What are those good thoughts?

A. Such as thoughts on the goodness of God, who grants me this day to labour in it for the salvation of my soul; and that perhaps this day may be my last.

O God my God, to Thee do I watch at break of day. For Thee my soul hath thirsted; for Thee my flesh, O how many ways! In a desert land, and where there is no way, and no water: so in the sanctuary have I come before Thee, to see Thy power and Thy glory (*Ps.* lxii. 2).

The kingdom of heaven is like to a householder, who went out early in the morning to hire labourers into his vineyard. And having agreed with the labourers for a penny a day, he sent them into his vineyard. And going out about the third hour, he saw others standing in the market-place idle. And he said to them: Go you also into my vineyard, and I will give you what shall be just. And they went their way. And again he went out about the sixth and the ninth hour: and did in like manner. But about the eleventh hour he went out and found others standing, and he saith to them: Why stand you here all the day idle? They say to him: Because no man hath hired us. He saith to them: Go you also into my vineyard. And when evening was come, the lord of the vineyard saith to his steward: Call the labourers and pay them their hire, beginning from the last even to the first (*S. Matt.* xx. 1).

I must work the works of him that sent me, whilst it is day: the night cometh when no man can work (_S. John_ ix. 4).

And I will say to my soul : Soul, thou hast much goods laid up for many years, take thy rest, eat, drink, make good cheer. But God said to him : Thou fool, this night do they require thy soul of thee ; and whose shall those things be which thou hast provided ? (_S. Luke_ xii. 19.)

From the morning watch even until night, let Israel hope in the Lord (_Ps._ cxxix. 6).

Q. And what should you do after you have put on your clothes ?

A. I should kneel down to my prayers, and perform my morning exercise.

If I have remembered Thee upon my bed, I will meditate on Thee in the morning : because Thou hast been my helper (_Ps._ lxii. 7).

From the rising of the sun even to the going down, My Name is great among the gentiles, and in every place there is sacrifice, and there is offered to My Name a clean oblation : for My Name is great among the gentiles, saith the Lord of hosts (_Mal._ i. 11).

I will wash my hands among the innocent : and will compass Thy altar, O Lord. That I may hear the voice of Thy praise : and tell of all Thy wondrous works. I have loved, O Lord, the beauty of Thy house : and the place where Thy glory dwelleth (_Ps._ xxv. 6).

Q. Should you do any thing more, if you have time and opportunity ?

A. Yes ; I should hear Mass and spend some time in meditation.

Q. What should you say when you begin any work or employment ?

A. O my God, I do this for the love of Thee.

And He said to them : How is it that you sought Me ? did you not know, that I must be about My Father's business ? (_S. Luke_ ii. 49.)

All whatsoever you do in word or in work, all things do ye in the Name of the Lord Jesus Christ, giving thanks to God and the Father by Him (_Col._ iii. 17).

Q. And what should you do as to your eating, drinking, sleeping, and diversion ?

A. I should use them

And the third day there was a marriage in Cana of Galilee : and the mother of Jesus was there. And with moderation, and do them to please God.

Q. What grace do you say before meals?
A. Bless us, O Lord, and these Thy gifts, which we are going to receive from Thy bounty, through Christ our Lord. Amen.

Q. What grace do you say after meals?
A. We give Thee thanks, Almighty God, for all Thy benefits, who livest and reignest, world without end. Amen. May the souls of the faithful, through the mercy of God, rest in peace. Amen.

Q. By what means should you sanctify your ordinary actions and employments of the day?
A. By often raising up my heart to God whilst I am about them, and saying some short prayer to Him.

Q. What should you do as often as you hear the clock strike?
A. I should turn myself to God, and say to Him, "O my God, teach

Jesus also was invited, and His disciples, to the marriage (*S. John* ii. 1).

The Lord appeared to him; and said unto him: I am the Almighty God: walk before Me, and be perfect (*Gen.* xvii. 1).
And the words of my mouth shall be such as may please: and the meditation of my heart always in Thy sight. O Lord, my helper and my redeemer (*Ps.* xviii. 15).
That they should seek God, if haply they may feel after Him or find Him, although He be not far from every one of us: for in Him we live and move and are: as some also of your own poets said (*Acts* xvii. 27).

My days have passed more swiftly than the web is cut by the weaver (*Job* vii. 6).
And immediately the cock crew. And Peter remembered the word of Jesus which He had said: Before

me to love Thee in time and eternity."

Q. What should you do as often as you receive any blessing from God?
A. I should immediately make Him a return of thanksgiving and love.

Q. What should you do when you find yourself tempted to sin?
A. I should make the sign of the cross upon my heart, and call upon God as earnestly as I can, saying, "Lord, save me, or I perish."

Q. And what if you have fallen into sin?
A. I should cast myself in spirit at the feet of Christ, and humbly beg His pardon, saying, "Lord, be merciful to me a sinner.

the cock crow, thou wilt deny Me thrice. And going forth he wept bitterly (*S. Matt.* xxvi. 74).

And Jesus answering, said: Were not ten made clean? and where are the nine? There is no one found to return and give glory to God, but this stranger. And He said to him: Arise, go thy way, for thy faith hath made thee whole (*S. Luke* xvii. 17).

But seeing the wind strong, he was afraid: and when he began to sink, he cried out, saying: Lord, save me. And immediately Jesus stretching forth His hand took hold of him, and said to him: O thou of little faith, why didst thou doubt? (*S. Matt.* xiv. 30.)

And as Jesus passed from thence, there followed Him two blind men crying out and saying, Have mercy on us, O Son of David (*S. Matt.* ix. 27).
And the publican standing afar off would not so much as lift up his eyes towards heaven; but struck his breast, saying: O God, be merciful to me a sinner (*S. Luke* xviii. 13).
I will arise, and will go to my Father, and say to Him: Father, I have sinned against heaven, and before thee: I am not now worthy to be called Thy son: make me as one of thy hired servants (*S. Luke* xv. 18).
And there came a leper to Him, beseeching Him, and kneeling down said to Him: If Thou wilt, Thou canst make me clean. And Jesus having compassion on him, stretched forth His hand; and touching him

saith to him : I will. Be thou made clean (*S. Mark* i. 40).

And behold a woman that was in the city, a sinner, when she knew that He sat at meat in the Pharisee's house, brought an alabaster box of ointment; and standing behind at His feet, she began to wash His feet with tears, and wiped them with the hairs of her head, and kissed His feet, and anointed them with the ointment (*S. Luke* vii. 37).

Wherefore I say to thee : Many sins are forgiven her, because she hath loved much. But to whom less is forgiven, he loveth less. And He said to her : Thy sins are forgiven thee (*S. Luke* vii. 47).

Q. What should you say when God sends you any cross, or suffering, or sickness, or pain?

A. I should say, "Lord, Thy will be done; I take this for my sins."

In those days Ezechias was sick even to death, and Isaias the son of Amos the prophet came unto him, and said to him : Thus saith the Lord : Take order with thy house, for thou shalt die and not live. And Ezechias turned his face toward the wall, and prayed to the Lord, and said : I beseech Thee, O Lord, remember how I have walked before Thee in truth, and with a perfect heart, and have done that which is good in Thy sight. And Ezechias wept with great weeping. And the word of the Lord came to Isaias, saying : Go and say to Ezechias : Thus saith the Lord the God of David thy father : I have heard thy prayer, and I have seen thy tears : behold I will add to thy days fifteen years (*Isa.* xxxviii. 1).

Q. And what other little prayers should you say to yourself from time to time in the day?

A. O Lord, teach me

Hear, O Lord, my prayer : and let my cry come to Thee. Turn not away Thy face from me : in the day when I am in trouble, incline Thy ear to me. In what day soever I to do Thy holy will in all things. Lord, keep me from sin. May the Name of our Lord be for ever blessed. Come, my dear Jesus, and take full possession of my soul. Glory be to the Father, and to the Son, and to the Holy Ghost. As it was in the beginning, is now, and ever shall be, world without end. Amen.

Q. What ought you to do before you go to bed?
A. I should kneel down and perform my evening exercise.

Q. How should you finish the day?
A. I should observe due modesty in going to bed; occupy myself with the thoughts of death; and endeavour to compose myself to rest at the foot of the cross, and to give my last thoughts to my crucified Saviour.

shall call upon Thee, hear me speedily (*Ps.* ci. 2).

As the hart panteth after the fountains of water: so my soul panteth after Thee, O God. My soul hath thirsted after the strong living God; when shall I come and appear before the face of God? *Ps.* xli. 2.

Let my prayer be directed as incense in Thy sight: the lifting up of my hands, as evening sacrifice. Set a watch, O Lord, before my mouth: and a door round about my lips. Incline not my heart to evil words; to make excuses in sins (*Ps.* cxl. 2).

Be ye angry, and sin not: the things you say in your hearts, be sorry for them upon your beds (*Ps.* iv. 5).
In peace in the self-same I will sleep, and I will rest: For Thou O Lord, singularly hast settled me in hope (*Ps.* iv. 9).
Into Thy hands I commend my spirit: Thou hast redeemed me, O Lord, the God of truth (*Ps.* xxx. 6).

APPENDIX.

INDEX OF TEXTS.

THE following "Index of Texts" is intended to give a short course of passages illustrating the Catechism which children may easily find out and learn. As far as I have seen, children can easily be led to take an interest in remembering a reasonable number of Scripture passages, appropriate to the Catechism they are learning; and I think that such a practice would be very useful to them, both intellectually and morally. It is arranged in three columns. 1. The different subjects the Catechism treats of, placed in order. 2. Two or three words of the text, chosen so as best to remind them of its bearing. 3. The reference to its place in the Scripture.

The texts referred to are all given in full in the earlier part of the book; but I think it well that children should sometimes, at least, try to find them for themselves, so as to know the context in which they occur, and understand the particular part applicable to the subject they are learning. The few words given may sometimes appear rather quaint, standing by themselves; but the object to be considered is, which words will best suggest the passage. Obviously, in many cases, the *first* words would not do so at all.

CHAPTER I.

SUBJECT.		REFERENCE.
Creation	Not we ourselves	Ps. xcix. 3.
Knowledge of God...	Eternal life...........................	S. John xvii. 3.
Service of God	With trembling ....,..............	Ps. ii. 11...
God our reward	Reward exceeding great	Gen. xv. 1.

Subject.		Reference.
Immortality............	Destroy both soul and body......	S. Matt. x. 28.
Care of our souls......	Seek ye first	S. Matt. vi. 33.
	For my sake	S. Luke ix. 24.
	A treasure hidden.................	S. Matt. xiii. 44
	Rust and moth	S. Matt. vi. 19.
	Thou fool, this night..............	S. Luke xii. 20.
Faith	O the depth	Rom. xi. 33.
	Overcometh the world	1 S. John v. 4.
Truth of God	Not as a man.......................	Num. xxiii. 19.
Necessity of revelation	Hid these things	S. Matt. xi. 25.
	No one knoweth.....................	S. Matt. xi. 27.
Testimony of the Church.	Shall be witnesses.................	Acts i. 8.
Authority of the Church.	He that heareth you	S. Luke x. 16.

CHAPTER II.

APOSTLES' CREED.

Self-existence of God	I am who I am	Exod. iii. 14.
	Life in Himself	S. John v. 26.
	Before Abraham	S. John viii. 58.
Majesty of God	An invincible King	Ecclus. xviii. 1.
	Nations before Him	Isa. xl. 17.
	What is man	Ps. viii. 5.
God the Creator and Preserver.	He spoke	Ps. xxxii. 9.
	For Thy will	Apoc. iv. 11.
	As a vesture	Heb. i. 12.
	If Thou turn away Thy face ...	Ps. ciii. 29.
Eternity of God	Alpha and Omega.................	Apoc. i. 8.
	A thousand years	2 S. Pet. iii. 8.
	Before the mountains..............	Ps. lxxxix. 2.
	As a pebble	Ecclus. xviii. 8.
God is every where...	If I ascend	Ps. cxxxviii. 7.
	In Him we live.....................	Acts xvii. 28.
Wisdom of God	O the depths	Rom. xi. 33.
	Say not I shall be hidden........	Ecclus. xvi. 16.
God is a Spirit	Spirit and truth	S. John iv. 24.

SUBJECT.		REFERENCE.
But one God	I alone am	Deut. xxxii. 39.
SECOND ART.		
Divinity of our Lord	The form of God	Phil. ii. 6.
	In the beginning	S. John i. 1:
	The Word was made flesh	S. John i. 14.
	Brightness of His glory............	Heb. i. 3.
	King of Israel......................	S. John i. 49.
Human nature of our Lord.	In all things like as we are	Heb. iv. 15.
	Handle and see	S. Luke xxiv. 39
	Made of a woman	Gal. iv. 4.
Christ our Redeemer	By whose stripes you were healed	1 S. Pet. ii. 24.
	Shall save His people	S. Matt. i. 21.
THIRD ART.		
Prophecies of the Incarnation.	Crush thy head	Gen. iii. 15.
	In thy seed.........................	Gen. xxii. 18.
	The sceptre	Gen. xlix. 10.
	A virgin shall conceive............	Isa. vii. 14.
	Sixty-two weeks....................	Dan. ix. 25.
Birth of Christ.........	This day is born....................	S. Luke ii. 10.
FOURTH ART.		
Prophecies of the Passion.	Be betrayed	S. Matt. xx. 18.
	Lifted up...........................	S. John xii. 32.
	To the slaughter	Isa. liii. 7.
The Crucifixion	The veil of the temple	S. Matt. xxvii. 51
Sign of the Cross ...	Sign of the Son of Man	S. Matt. xxiv. 30
	God forbid that I should glory	Gal. vi. 14.
FIFTH ART.		
Descent of the Lord into Limbo.	Abraham's bosom	S. Luke xvi. 22.
	Spirits in prison.....................	1 S. Pet. iii. 19.
The Resurrection ...	Jonas the prophet	S. Matt. xii. 39.
	Ought not Christ	S. Luke xxiv. 26
	Preaching vain	1 Cor. xv. 14.
	First fruits of the dead	1 Cor. xv. 20.
SIXTH ART.		
The Ascension.........	He must reign	1 Cor. xv. 25.
	Right hand of God	Colos. iii. 1.
SEVENTH ART.		
Judgment..............	Taken up from you	Acts i. 11.
	The sheep from the goats.........	S. Matt. xxv. 32
	They that pierced Him............	Apoc. i. 7.
	Every idle word....................	S. Matt. xii. 36.

SUBJECT.		REFERENCE.
Hell	The tip of his finger	S. Luke xvi. 24.
	Pool of fire	Apoc. xx. 15.
	Smoke of their torments	Apoc. xiv. 11.
	Their worm shall not die.........	Isa. lxvi. 24.
	Torment of brimstone	Isa. xxx. 33.
Heaven.................	Eye hath not seen	1 Cor. ii. 9.
	God shall wipe away...............	Apoc. xxi. 4.
	The lamp thereof	Apoc. xxi. 23.
EIGHTH ART.		
The Holy Ghost	Spirit of truth........................	S. John xvi. 13.
	Bring back to your minds.........	S. John xiv. 26.
	It is not you that speak	S. Matt. x. 20.
NINTH ART.		
The whole Church ...	Mount Sion	Heb. xii. 22.
	Under His feet	Eph. i. 22.
Prophecies of the Visible Church.	The top of mountains	Isa. ii. 2.
	Stone without hands..............	Dan. ii. 34.
	Shall stand for ever	Dan. ii. 44.
Supremacy of S. Peter.	On this rock	S. Matt. xvi. 18.
	Feed My lambs	S. John xxi. 15.
	Sift you as wheat	Luke xxii. 31.
Christ's Church on earth visible.	One fold...	S. John x. 16.
	Net cast into the sea..............	S. Matt. xiii. 47.
	One body	Eph. iv. 4.
Christ's Church an organized body.	The body of Christ	Eph. iv. 11.
	Placed you bishops	Acts xx. 28.
	Account of your souls	Heb. xiii. 17.
Unity of the Church	Keep them in My Name	S. John xvii. 11.
	Baptized into one body...........	1 Cor. xii. 13.
Holiness	Not having spot.....................	Eph. v. 27.
Catholicity	To every creature	S. Mark xvi. 15.
	Come from afar	Isa. lx. 4.
	Tribes, peoples, and tongues ...	Apoc. vii. 9.
Apostolicity............	I also send you	S. John xx. 21.
	Unless they be sent	Rom. x. 15.
Authority of the Church.	Go and teach	S. Matt. xxviii. 19
	Heareth Me	S. Luke x. 16.
	Tell the Church....................	S. Matt. xviii. 17.
	Pillar and ground	1 Tim. iii. 15
Intercession of Saints	Wrath be kindled	Exod. xxxii. 10.
	How long, O Lord ?...............	Apoc. vi. 9.
	Much incense.......................	Apoc. viii. 3.

SUBJECT.		REFERENCE.
Purgatory..............	The last farthing	S. Matt. v. 25.
	So as by fire	1 Cor. iii. 14.
TENTH ART.		
Original Sin...........	By one man ....—...	Rom. v. 12.
Actual Sin	If we say............................	1 S. John i. 8.
	The wages of sin	Rom. vi. 23.
	A man shall sow	Gal. vi. 7.
	Patient rewarder	Ecclus. v. 4.
ELEVENTH ART.		
Resurrection of the body.	The dead shall hear	S. John v. 25.
	At the last trumpet	1 Cor. xv. 51.
TWELFTH ART.		
Life everlasting	Wash their robes	Apoc. xxii. 14.

CHAPTER III.

THE LORD'S PRAYER.

Necessity of faith ...	Without faith.......................	Heb. xi. 6.
	Overcometh the world	1 S. John v. 4.
Good works...........	Dead in itself.....................	S. James ii. 17.
	Calling and election	2 Pet. i. 10.
Necessity of grace ...	No man can say....................	1 Cor. xii. 3.
	Am what I am	1 Cor. xv. 10.
	Except the Father.................	S. John vi. 44.
	Without me	S. John xv. 5.
	Unless the Lord...................	Ps. cxxvi. 1.
Sufficiency of grace...	Above that which you are able	1 Cor. x. 13.
	Perfect in infirmity	2 Cor. xii. 9.
Prayer	Prayer is good	Tobias xii. 8.
	Before prayer.....................	Eclus. xviii. 23.
	Ask amiss	S. James iv. 3.
Our Father	As a father.........................	Ps. cii. 13.
	Where is my honour ?	Mal. i. 6.
Hallowed be Thy Name.	How admirable	Ps. viii. 2.
	Not to us	Ps. cxiii. 9.
Thy Kingdom come (*Heaven*).	The just shall shine	S. Matt. xiii. 43.

SUBJECT.		REFERENCE.
The Church	A grain of mustard seed	S.Matt.xiii.31.
Grace	Within you...........................	S. Luke xvii. 21
Thy Will be done ...	Not as I will	S. Matt. xxvi. 39
Daily Bread............	The young ravens	Ps. cxlvi. 9.
Our trespasses.........	Leave there thy offering	S. Matt. v. 23.
Temptation	Loveth danger	Ecclus. iii. 27.
Deliver us from evil	Fall at thy side	Ps. xc. 7.
Angels	Ministering spirits	Heb. i. 14.
	Face of My Father	S.Matt.xviii.10
The B. Virgin Mary	All generations	S. Luke i. 48.

CHAPTER IV.

THE TEN COMMANDMENTS.

Obligation of the Commandments.	A sign on your hands	Deut. xi. 18.
	Truth is not in him	1 S. John ii. 4.
	Guilty of all	S. James ii. 10.
Avoid evil and do good	Broken cisterns	Jer. ii. 13.
First Commandment	Greatest and first	S. Matt. xxii.36
Idolatry	Mouths and speak not	Ps. cxiii. 4.
	Offspring of God	Acts xvii. 29.
False religion	Strange fire........................	Levit. x. 1.
	An Angel from heaven............	Gal. i. 8.
	Sound words	2 Tim. i. 13.
Sacrilege	Arose a leprosy	2 Paral. xxvi. 19
Dealing with the Devil	A God in Israel....................	4 Kings i. 3.
Superstition............	Deceitful divination	Eclus. xxxiv. 5.
Images	Cherubim and palm trees.........	3 Kings vi. 29.
	Brazen serpent	Num. xxi. 8.
Honour to saints ...	To and fro	Wisd. iii. 7.
	Twelve seats	S. Matt. xix. 27.
Relics, &c.	The mantle of Elias	4 Kings ii. 13.
	The bones of Eliseus...............	4 Kings xiii. 21.
	Handkerchiefs and aprons	Acts xix. 12.

SUBJECT.		REFERENCE.
Blaspheming, cursing, &c.	Hold him guiltless................,...	Exod. xx. 7.
	He that blasphemeth...............	Levit. xxiv. 16.
	Neither by heaven...............,......	S.James v. 12.
Observance of Sunday	Keep you My Sabbath	Exod. xxxi. 14.
	Lord of the Sabbath...............	S. Matt. xii. 8.
Duty of children, &c.	Commandment with a promise	Eph. vi. 1.
	Layeth up a treasure...............	Ecclus. iii. 5.
	Lamp shall be put out	Prov. xx. 20.
	Every creature for God's sake ...	1 S. Pet. ii. 13.
	Not serving to the eye	Eph. vi. 5.
	Serve the altar	1 Cor. ix. 13.
	Account of your souls	Heb. xiii. 17.
Duty of parents, &c.	Provoke not	Eph. vi. 4.
	Forbearing threatenings ....·..	Eph. vi. 9.
	A son ill taught.....................	Ecclus. xxii. 3.
Murder.................	Thy brother's blood	Gen. iv. 10.
	His blood shall be shed	Gen. ix. 6.
Anger, hatred, and revenge.	Angry, and sin not	Eph. iv. 26.
	Hateth his brother..................	1 S.John iii. 15.
	Not revenging yourselves.........	Rom. xii. 19.
	Seeketh to revenge	Eclus. xxviii. 1.
Scandal	Wo to that man.......................	S.Matt.xviii. 7.
	Weak brother perish...............	1 Cor. viii. 11.
Sixth Commandment	God is not mocked	Gal. vi. 7.
	The chaste generation	Wisd. iv. 1.
Stealing, &c.	He that stole	Eph. iv. 28.
	Let none of you suffer	1 S. Pet. iv. 15.
Lying	Judge not	S. Luke vi. 37.
	Lying lips	Prov. xii. 22.
	Leaven of the Pharisees	S. Luke xii. 1.
Concupiscence.........	Every man is tempted	S. James i. 14.
	Pride of life	1 S.John ii. 16.

———◆———

CHAPTER V.

THE COMMANDMENTS OF THE CHURCH.

Fasting.................	When you fast	S. Matt. vi. 16.
	Then they shall fast	S. Mark ii. 20.
	Is not cast out........................	S. Matt. xvii.20
	Rend your hearts	Joel ii. 13.

SUBJECT.		REFERENCE.
Mortification	Let him deny himself	S. Luke ix. 23.
	I chastise my body	I Cor. ix. 25.
	Suffereth violence	S. Matt. xi. 12.

———◆———

CHAPTER VI.

THE SACRAMENTS.

Baptism	Baptizing them	S. Matt. xxviii. 19
	One baptism	Eph. iv. 5.
	Have put on Christ	Gal. iii. 27.
	Wash away thy sins	Acts xxii. 16.
Confirmation	The Apostles who were in Jerusalem	Acts viii. 14.
Holy Eucharist	If any man eat	S. John vi. 51.
	I have received of the Lord	I Cor. xi. 23.
	The chalice of benediction	I Cor. x. 16.
	In the strength of that food......	3 Kings xix. 8.
	The hidden manna	Apoc. ii. 17.
	Nation so great	Deut. iv. 7.
The Mass...............	Standing as it were slain	Apoc. v. 6.
	Priest for ever	Heb. vii. 17.
	From the rising of the sun	Mal. i. 11.
	Who shall ascend	Ps. xxiii. 3.
	Thy altars, O Lord	Ps. lxxxiii. 4.
Penance	Whose sins..........................	S. John xx. 23.
	Whatsoever you shall bind	S. Matt. xviii. 18
	Is it easier to say	S. Matt. ix. 5.
Contrition	An afflicted spirit	Ps. l. 19.
	If the wicked do penance.........	Ezec. xviii. 21.
	I will recount to Thee	Isa. xxxviii. 15.
	Say not, "I have sinned"	Ecclus. v. 4.
Extreme Unction ...	Anointed with oil	S. Mark vi. 12.
Holy Order	Neglect not the grace	I Tim. iv. 14.
	Obey your prelates	Heb. xiii. 17.
	The lips of the priest	Mal. ii. 7.
Matrimony	Subject to their husbands..	Eph. v. 22.

CHAPTER VII.

VIRTUES AND VICES.

SUBJECT.		REFERENCE.
Faith, Hope, and Charity.	Now there remain.................	1 Cor. xiii. 13.
	A light shining in a dark place	2 Pet. i. 19.
	Substance of things	Heb. xi. 1.
	Without Faith	Heb. xi. 6.
	In Thee, O Lord	Ps. xxx. 2.
	As Mount Sion	Ps. cxxiv. 1.
	I will still give praise	Ps. xli. 6.
	My body to be burned	1 Cor. xiii. 3.
	If any man love not	1 Cor. xvi. 22.
	Let us therefore love..............	1 S. John iv. 19.
	Height nor depth	Rom. viii. 38.
Cardinal Virtues	The wisdom of the flesh	Rom. viii. 6.
	Not to be more wise..............	Rom. xii. 3.
Works of Mercy	Cup of cold water.................	S. Matt. x. 42.
	If a brother or sister..............	S. James ii. 15.
	In word nor in tongue	1 S. John iii. 18.
	Hide the dead by day	Tobias xii. 12.
	Instruct such an one..............	Gal. vi. 1.
Eight Beatitudes......	Shall hardly enter.................	S. Matt. xix. 23
Deadly Sins............	Be humbled therefore	1 S. Peter v. 5.
	This was the iniquity of Sodom	Ezech. xvi. 49.
	Crieth to me from the earth......	Gen. iv. 10.
	The hire of the labourers	S. James v. 4.
	My secret sins	Ps. xviii. 13.
Eminent good works	Delivereth from death	Tobias xii. 9.
Four last things	In all thy works...................	Ecclus. vii. 40.
	Unless the grain of wheat	S. John xii. 24.
	The dead, great and small	Apoc. xx. 12.

- done

CHAPTER VIII.

THE CHRISTIAN'S RULE OF LIFE.

SUBJECT.		REFERENCE.
Christian's Rule of Life	I am the Way	S. John xiv. 6.
Hatred of Sin and love of God.	The face of a serpent That He should be loved	Ecclus. xxi. 2. S. Mark xii. 33.
Love of our neighbour	For all the law	Gal. v. 14.
Self-denial	Wide is the gate Whosoever doth not carry My yoke is sweet	S. Matt. vii. 13. S. Luke xiv. 27 S. Matt. xi. 28.
The Devil	Be sober and watch	1 S. Pet. v. 8.
The World	Love not the world	1 S. John ii. 15.
The Flesh	Walk in the Spirit	Gal. v. 16.
Watching and Prayer	Watch and pray Be subject therefore	S. Matt. xxvi. 41 S. James iv. 7.
Dependence on God	Unless the Lord	Ps. cxxvi. 1.

CHAPTER IX.

THE CHRISTIAN'S DAILY EXERCISE.

| Christian's Daily Exercise. | To thee do I watch
From the morning watch
If I have remembered
All whatsoever you do
O thou of little faith
The Publican standing afar off
Many sins are forgiven
Father, I have sinned
Let my prayer
In peace in the self-same
Into Thy hands | Ps. lxii. 2.
Ps. cxxix. 6.
Ps. lxii. 7.
Colos. iii. 17.
Matt. xiv. 30.
S. Luke xviii. 13
S. Luke vii. 47.
S. Luke xv. 18.
Ps. cxl. 2.
Ps. iv. 9.
Ps. xxx. 6. |

NOTES.

NOTE A, p. 24.

TESTIMONY OF THE FATHERS TO THE ANCIENT USE OF THE SIGN OF THE CROSS.

THIS "sign of the Son of Man" has always been considered to be the sign of the Cross. The use of this sign has prevailed in the Church from the very beginning of Christianity to the present day.

Tertullian, who was nearly the earliest of the Fathers, and lived in the second century, describes the use of it as a custom then universal and firmly established in the Church. His words are, "In all our travels and movements, in all our coming in and going out, in putting on our clothes and shoes, at the bath, at the table, in lighting our lamps, in lying down, in sitting down, whatever employment occupies us, we mark our foreheads with the sign of the cross. For these and such like rules, if thou requirest the law in the Scriptures, thou shalt find none : superstition will be pleaded to thee as originating, custom as confirming, and faith as observing them."—*De Coron. Mil.* n. 3, 4.

Again, St. Cyril of Jerusalem, in the fourth century, says, "Let us not, therefore, be ashamed of the cross of Christ ; but even though another hide it, do thou openly seal it on thy brow, that the devils, beholding that royal sign, may flee far away trembling. But make thou this sign when thou eatest and drinkest, sittest or liest down, risest up, speakest, walkest ; in a word, on every occasion ; for He who was here crucified is above in the heavens."—*Catech.* iv. n. 14, p. 58.

See "Faith of Catholics attested by the Fathers of the First Five Centuries," by Rev. James Waterworth.—Vol. iii. pp. 430—433.

NOTE B, p. 35.

THE SUPREMACY OF THE POPE IN THE EARLY CHURCH.

In these passages our Lord compares His Church to a house, and makes S. Peter the foundation of it ; to a flock, and makes him the shepherd of it ; and then, without figure, gives him the office of confirming his brethren with a distinct guarantee that *his* faith shall not fail.

This antecedent proof of the supremacy of S. Peter and his successors corresponds accurately with the subsequent history of the Church.

1. We find S. Peter, immediately on the ascension of his Master, taking on himself the guidance of the Church. He, on all occasions, speaks for his brethren, and puts the *first hand* to every undertaking.

2. The Popes, from the beginning, assumed a like authority. We find the Popes of the first five centuries using very much the tone which Pope Pius IX. uses at this day ; and we find illustrious bishops, of the most important sees in the world, acquiescing without a murmur. For instance, Pope S. Julius, in the fourth century, says, " And why were we not written to concerning the Church, especially of Alexandria ? or, are you ignorant that this has been the custom, first to write to us, and thus what is just be decreed from this place ? If, therefore, any suspicion fell on the bishop there, it was befitting to write to this Church."—*Ep. ad Eusebium,* n. 21, p. 13.

S. Damasus, another Pope in the same century, says, " Although, dearest brethren, the decrees of the Fathers are known to you, yet we cannot wonder at your carefulness as regards the institutes of our forefathers, that you cease not, as custom has ever been, to refer all those things which can admit of any doubt to us, as to the head, that thence you may derive answers whence you received the institution and rule of living rightly. . . . . Not that you are in any way deficient in knowledge of the law of the Church ; but that, supported by the authority of the Apostolic See, you may not deviate in any thing from its regulations. . . . . It does with reason concern us, who ought to hold the chief government in the Church, if we by our silence favour error."—*Epis.* v. *Prospero Numid. et aliis.*

S. Innocent I., Pope in the fifth century, says, " After having caused your letter to be several times read to me, I noticed that a kind of injury was done to the Apostolic See, unto which, as unto the head of the Churches, that statement was sent—the sentence of that See being still treated as doubtful. The renewed questioning contained in your report compels me, therefore, to repeat in plainer terms the subjects concerning which I remember having written to you."—*Ep.* xvii. n. 1.

Pope S. Boniface, also in the fifth century, says, " The institution of the Universal Church took its beginning from the honour bestowed on Blessed Peter, in whom its government and headship reside. For from him, as its source, did ecclesiastical discipline flow over all the Churches when the culture of religion had begun to make progress. The precepts of the Synod of Nicæa bear no other testimony ; insomuch that that Synod did not attempt to make any regulations in his regard, as it saw that nothing could be conferred that was superior to his own dignity : it knew, in fine, that every thing had been bestowed on him by the word of the Lord. It is, therefore, certain that this Church is, to the Churches spread over the whole world, as the head is to its members ; from which Church whoso has cast himself off, becomes an alien from the Christian religion, whereas he has begun not to be in the same bonds of fellowship."—*Ep.* xiv. *Epis. Thess.*

Could the present Pope assert his right with less ceremony or more conclusiveness?

3. Not only did the Popes assert their authority, but the Church admitted it.

S. Irenæus, in the second century, says, "To this Church [Rome], on account of a more powerful principality, it is necessary that every Church, that is, those who are on every side faithful, resort, in which [Church] always by those, who are on every side, has been preserved the tradition which is from Apostles."—*Adv. hæres.*

S. Ambrose, Archbishop of Milan in the fourth century, says, "We have recognized in the letter of your Holiness the watchfulness of the good shepherd, who dost faithfully keep the gate entrusted to thee ; and with pious solicitude dost guard the fold of Christ, worthy, indeed that the Lord's sheep should hear and follow thee. . . . . Those, therefore, whom your Holiness has condemned, know that, amongst us also, they have been, according to your judgment, condemned."—*Ep.* xcii. *Siricio.*

S. Jerome says (fourth century), "Following no chief but Christ, I am joined in communion with your Holiness, that is, with the chair of Peter. Upon that rock I know that the Church is built. Whosoever eats the Lamb out of this house is profane. If any be not in the ark of Noah, he will perish whilst the deluge prevaileth." Again he says, "The Church here is rent into three parts, each of which is eager to drag me to itself. . . . . Meanwhile I cry aloud, 'If any one is united to the chair of S. Peter, he is mine.' Meletius, Vitalis, and Paulinus, all assert that they adhere to thee. I might assent if only one of them declared this : as it is, either two or all of them are liars. Wherefore, I beseech your Holiness, by the cross of our Lord, that—as you follow the Apostles in honour, you may follow them also in merit—you would, by your letter, make known to me with whom I ought to hold communion in Syria."— *Ep.* xv., xvi. *ad Damas. Papam.*

S. John Chrysostom, Patriarch of Constantinople, also in the fourth century, says, "Christ, speaking to the leader of the Apostles, says, 'Peter, lovest thou Me?' and upon his affirming that he did, He replies, 'If thou lovest Me, feed My sheep.' . . . . Why did Christ shed His blood ? That He might obtain possession of those very sheep which He entrusted to Peter and to his successors."— *De Sacerd.*

S. Augustin, Bishop of Hippo in the fifth century, says, "That city [Carthage] had a bishop of no slight authority, who was able not to heed the multitude of enemies conspiring against him, when he saw himself united by letters of communion, both with the Roman Church, in which the primacy of the Apostolic Chair has always been in force, and with other lands."—*Ep.* xliii.

He also says, "In the Catholic Church . . . . the succession of priests, from the very Chair of the Apostle Peter—to whom the Lord, after His resurrection, committed His sheep to be fed—down even to the present bishop, keeps me."—*Contr. Ep. Fund. Manich.*

We may add the words addressed by the Pope's legate to the Council of Ephesus in the fifth century :—"It is a matter of doubt to none, yea, rather it is a thing known to all ages, that the holy and most blessed Peter, the prince and head of the Apostles, the pillar of the faith, the foundation of the Catholic Church, received the keys of the kingdom from Jesus Christ, our Lord and Saviour and Redeemer of mankind. And to him was given authority to bind and loose sins : who even till this present, and always, both lives and judges in his successors. Our holy and most blessed Pope Celestin, the bishop, the canonical successor, and vicegerent of this Peter, has sent us as representatives of his person."— *Concil. Eph. Act.* iii.

When we consider that the Fathers who speak thus of the Pope's authority were themselves men of the greatest weight in their day, from position and talents, we may reasonably conclude that the Church then accepted the assertion of the Pope's authority in much the same way in which she accepts it now—that is, with the respect and obedience due to an authority established by God.

These passages may be found respectively at pp. 70, 74, 80, 89, 64, 76, 78, 80, 85, 84 of Waterworth's " Faith of Catholics " (vol. ii.), where a great number of similar ones may be read.

NOTE C, p. 98.

ON THE REAL PRESENCE.

There are very few subjects on which the Holy Scriptures speak with such clearness as they do about the Real Presence of our Lord in the Holy Eucharist.

We have, first, the promise of our Lord whilst He was yet with His apostles (S. John vi.). Second, the words of Institution when this promise was fulfilled. Third, the reference made to it by S. Paul years after, when the Holy Eucharist had become the daily practice of the Church, in which he repeats these same words of Institution, and draws from them consequences which could only follow from the doctrine of the Real Presence. " He that eateth and drinketh unworthily, eateth and drinketh judgment to himself, not *discerning the Body of the Lord."* In all these places the same truth is declared in the very plainest of words, without the remotest hint at any figurative explanation. If these words do not express it, let us ask what words would ? Is it *possible* for words to convey the Catholic doctrine more clearly than these do ?—at least, putting aside those words which have since acquired a technical and controversial sense.

The Fathers, too, abound in the clearest possible passages on this subject. I will give one specimen of their language from S. Ambrose. He says, " Now if a human benediction availed so much to change nature, what shall we say concerning the Divine Consecration itself, where the very words of the Lord, the Saviour, operate ? For this sacrament, which thou receivest, is effected by the word of Christ. Now if the word of Elias so availed as to draw down fire from heaven, shall not the word of Christ be of avail to change the natures of elements ? Concerning the works of the whole world, you have read that 'He spoke and they were made, He commanded and they were created.' The word, therefore, of Christ, which could out of nothing make that which was not—cannot it change those things which are into that which they were not ? For to give new natures to things is not less than to change their natures. . . . The Lord Jesus himself cries out, ' This is My body.' Before the benediction of heavenly words, another species is named; after the consecration His Body is signified. Himself declares it His own Blood. Before the consecration it is called another thing; after consecration it is called blood. And thou sayest, Amen; that is, it is true. What the mouth speaks, let the inward mind confess : what language expresses, let thought feel."—See Waterworth's "Faith of Catholics" (vol. ii. pp. 297, 298).

Perhaps, however, the most striking testimony to the faith of the early Church comes from the ancient Liturgies, of which mention will be made in the Note on the Mass.

NOTE D, p. 104.

THE ANCIENT LITURGIES ON THE REAL PRESENCE.

Besides the Latin "Mass," there are, both in the Church and in schismatical bodies out of the Church, a number of other "Liturgies," or forms, in which the Eucharistic Sacrifice is offered up. These present, perhaps, the most remarkable proof of the Doctrine of the Real Presence.

They are of the highest antiquity, going up, as far as can be traced, to the times of the Apostles. They vary very considerably in ritual; that is, they are celebrated in different languages, and use different forms of words. The ceremonies employed, and the vestments worn, are also widely different. Nevertheless in substance they perfectly agree. Their testimony to the faith of the early Church about the Real Presence is unanimous, and is set forth, for the most part, in language far more striking than that employed by the Roman Mass.

It will be interesting to quote the account of the origin of these Liturgies given by S. Proclus, a father of the fifth century.

He says, "Many other individuals, and they divine pastors and teachers of the Church, who have succeeded the Sacred Apostles, have left in writing, and delivered to the Church, the exposition of the mystic liturgy. Of these, the first and most celebrated are blessed Clement, the disciple and successor of the Coryphæus of the Apostles, the Apostles themselves dictating to him" [he then mentions S. James of Jerusalem and S. Basil, who, he says, abbreviated the former liturgy]. "After our Saviour was taken up into heaven, the Apostles, before being scattered over the whole world, being together in oneness of mind, passed whole days in prayer; and having found the mystic Sacrifice of the Lord's Body a great consolation, they sang it at very great length; for this, and teaching, they considered preferable to any thing else. With very great gladness and much joy were they instant in this Divine Sacrifice, ever bearing in mind the Lord's words, which He says, '*This is My body;*' and '*Do this in memory of Me;*' and '*He that eateth My flesh and drinketh My Blood, abideth in Me and I in him.*' For this cause, too, with a contrite heart, they sang many prayers, earnestly imploring the Divine aid. . . . . Through those prayers they expected the advent of the Holy Ghost, that by His own Divine Presence He might make and exhibit the bread that lay there for a sacrifice, and the wine mixed with water, that very same Body and Blood of our Lord Jesus Christ; which is no less done even to this day, and will be done even to the consummation of the world." [He adds that S. John Chrysostom, to meet the degeneracy of the times, also abridged the Liturgy.] "For this cause he also omitted much, and arranged it to be celebrated in a conciser form, for fear lest, by degrees, men who are specially fond of a kind of liberty and ease, deluded by the deceitful reasonings of the enemy, might keep aloof from so great an Apostolical and Divine tradition." — *Tract. de Traditione Divinæ Missæ.*

It appears that the Liturgies were generally committed to writing about the middle of the fourth century. Up till that time, that is, in the days of persecution, they had been handed down by unwritten tradition, on account of that fear in which the early Church lived lest holy things should fall into the hands of the pagans.

There are three great sources from which are derived the numerous Liturgies in use in the Christian Church :—

1. That of S. James the Apostle, the first Bishop of Jerusalem, which is chiefly followed by the Oriental Churches.

2. That of S. Mark the Evangelist. S. Mark was the disciple of S. Peter, and Bishop of Alexandria. This is followed by the Ethiopian Liturgy used in Africa.

3. That of S. Peter, used in the Latin Churches.

These Liturgies all contain,—

1. Prayers for the dead.

2. A narrative of the institution of the Holy Eucharist—which is almost word for word the same in every Liturgy, except the Ethiopian, and yet is not taken from any of the Scripture accounts.

3. A prayer that God will make, or change, the bread and wine into the Body and Blood of Christ.

4. They declare that a mystery and sacrifice are celebrated, and they contain an actual sacrificial oblation.

5. Generally they mention the mixture of water with the wine.

6. The sign of the cross.

I will quote now a few expressions from some of these Liturgies to show how vivid a belief in the Real Presence is expressed in them.

In the Alexandrian Liturgy of S. Basil the priest elevates the larger part of the consecrated Host, and says," The holy body and precious true blood of Jesus Christ the Son of God." The people answer, " Amen." *Priest.*—" The holy precious body and true blood of Jesus Christ the Son of God." *People.*—" Amen." *Priest.*— " Body and blood of Emmanuel our God, this is truly. Amen." *People.*—" Amen. I believe, I believe and confess, till my last breath, that it is the very life-giving flesh of Thine only-begotten Son, but our Lord and God and 'Saviour Jesus Christ."—*Waterworth*, vol. ii. p. 186.

In the Liturgy of S. Gregory the Illuminator we find : " Thou hast granted unto us, lowly men and sinners, and Thine unworthy servants, confidence to stand at Thy holy altar, and to offer up to Thee the awful and unbloody sacrifice, for our own sins, and the ignorances of Thy people, for the pardon and rest of our fathers and brethren who have already fallen asleep."—*Ib.* p. 190.

The Æthiopian Liturgy, called that' of S. Cyril, says, " Have mercy, O Lord, on the souls of thy servants, who have eaten thy body, and drunk thy blood, and received rest in Thy faith."—*Ib.* p. 191.

The same Liturgy has also the following testimony to the *worship* due to our Lord in the Holy Sacrament :—

" Hosts of Angels stand before the Saviour of the world, and surround the body and blood of our Lord and Saviour Jesus Christ : let us approach before His presence and venerate Christ with faith."—*Ib.* p. 192.

Also it says, " The holy, precious, living, and true body of our Lord and Saviour Jesus Christ, which is given for remission of sins, and everlasting life to those who receive it with faith. Amen. . . .

" This is, in real truth, the body and blood of Emmanuel. Amen. I believe, I believe, I believe, from this time forth, now, and for evermore. Amen. This is the body and blood of our Lord and Saviour Jesus Christ, which He received of the Lady of us all, the holy and pure Virgin Mary.—*Ib.* p. 192.

Quotations in the same strain might be continued to a great length. They may be found in the book already mentioned, " Faith of Catholics " (vol. ii.), pages above given.

May we not then say, if the faith of the Catholic Church *now* about the Holy Eucharist and the Mass was *not* that of the Apostles, let us hear how it is that the same faith is so vividly impressed on every line of the earliest Christian liturgical records in all parts of the world, and breathes, if we may so say, from the very heart of the early Church !

NOTE E, p. 113.

CONFESSION.

The testimony of the fathers to the practice of confession is singularly full and clear. It begins, too, with almost the earliest fathers of both East and West.

Tertullian, in the second century, says, " Brave thou art in thy modesty, truly ! bearing an open front in sinning, and a bashful one in praying for pardon ! . . . . . Is it better to be damned in secret than absolved openly ? It is a miserable thing to come to confession. . . . . It is a miserable thing to be cut and burnt with cautery. . . . . Nevertheless, those things which heal by unpleasant means excuse likewise, by the benefit of the cure, their own offensiveness. . . . ."—*Faith of Catholics*, vol. iii. p. 42.

" If thou drawest back from confession, consider in thy heart that hell-fire which confession shall quench for thee. . . . .

" When, therefore, thou knowest that, against hell-fire, after that first protection of baptism ordained by the Lord, there is yet in confession a second aid, why dost thou abandon thy salvation ? . . . ." —*Ib.* p. 43.

In the third century Origen, the great doctor of the early Greek

Church, says, " So also they who have sinned, if they conceal and retain the sin within them, they are oppressed within and almost suffocated. . . . . But if a man becomes his own accuser, while he accuses himself and confesses, he at the same time ejects the sin, and at the same time digests the whole cause of the disease. Only look diligently round to whom thou oughtest to confess thy sin. Prove first the physician . . . . who knows how to be weak with the weak. . . . . If he shall have understood and foresee, that thy sickness is such as ought to be set forth and cured in the assembly of the whole Church, and, thereby, perhaps, others be edified, and thou thyself easily cured, this must be prescribed with much delibe- ration, and on the very experienced advice of that physician."— *Ib.* p. 48.

This quotation clearly proves that the confession referred to was not *necessarily* a *public* confession, but *private* confession, such as it is now the discipline of the Church to employ.

The following shows that confession was not confined to notorious or even grievous sins. S. Cyprian, in the fourth century, says, " How much loftier in faith, and in fear of God superior, are they who, though implicated in no crime of sacrifice or of accepting a certifi- cate [1], yet, because they have only had thought thereof, this very sin sorrowingly and honestly confessing before the priests of God, make a confession of their conscience, expose the burthen of the soul, seek out a salutary cure even for light and little wounds."— *Ib.* p. 52.

I must again refer the reader to the " Faith of Catholics " (vol. iii.), where testimonies of the Fathers breathing the same spirit are quoted at great length.

---

[1] Referring to those who had fallen away in time of persecution, and either sacrificed to idols or pretended to do so, and saved themselves by receiving certificates from the pagan authorities that they had sacrificed.

FINIS.

R. WASHBOURNE, PRINTER, 18A, PATERNOSTER ROW.